The Hour before Morning

Arwen Spicer

Dedication
To Aaron. In 1996, you were this story's first reader and have
been its staunch supporter ever since. Thank you!

Acknowledgments
Aaron Williams
Geoffrey Aguirre
Daphne Gabrieli
Sasha Tavenner Kruger
Nye Joell Hardy
Camille Picott
Mallory
Stephen Gold
Ann Wilkes
Kim Richards
Rachel Fellman

And last but never least, my mother, Patricia Spicer

Without your suggestions, corrections, proofreading, and belief
in this novel, it would not be the work I am proud of today. My
sincerest thanks to all of you.

Special thanks to Tiffany Christian for writing the Rha-Rhyd
workers' song.

CHAPTER ONE

People of Ash'tor, I know you are not evil. You
are human, and like most of us humans, you
strive to do good. I know this; I am, after all, to
some extent, one of you. I believe that most of
you support the absorption of the Outlying
Planets, at least in part, from a desire to improve
living conditions on these worlds. Yet your
attempts to incorporate us into your Nation can
only succeed by our murder. For we Outliers do
not wish to be you, and we will not submit to
you. You may call us fools for that. The fact
remains: we will not submit. I must ask you then:
is the salvation you offer us worth more than our
lives?

Letter to the Nine Ministries of Ash'tor, 2109 A.E.
by Denned Jenchae. Received in Ash'tor three
months before his arrest on Taenquûn

Jenchae did not want, in his final hours, to go back to
being what he had been. He had consecrated his life to
overcoming his hatred for Ash'tor. Yet here, on this prison ship,
in the black-walled bareness of this cell, he knew he had not
overcome it.

No more thoughts: only the floor against his back, his
hands on his chest. From the ceiling, twilight lamps looked
down like facets of an insect's eye. The ventilation system
whistled airily.

He jerked at the grind of the cell door rolling open, a
sound he'd have recognized in his sleep, though he'd only ever
heard it when he'd entered this cell.

Since that day, the ship had been still, grounded at the space port, not even en route for the Death Planet yet. It could not be his time to die. . .

Whiteness flared into the room. A weapon?

Just the light from the corridor, normal illumination slicing the cell's honeyed brown.

A yearning to dash into that light flooded him — and a terror of the ones who barred the way: a slight man in black prison coveralls and a guard behind him, gun at the ready. Jenchae sensed fear leaking through a closed mind. The guard's, he realized with a start. The guard was afraid.

By a force of will, Jenchae steadied himself. Over the protest of arthritic joints, he sat up, outwardly composed.

The guard pushed the prisoner into the cell.

A dangerous man. Or dangerous only to Ash'torian domination?

The door clanked shut, plunging the cell into darkness. As his eyes readjusted to gloom, Jenchae stood. The newcomer was looking at him darkly — no, not at him: at the place.

The stranger was a sverra: a species engineered from humans but stronger and longer-lived. He had a sverra's eyes, black, too large, and a sverra's white, gleaming skin. Yet he was also part human, his hair a human shade: blond or brown — hard to tell in the dimness.

And he's here. The simple fact struck with the force of revelation. *He's here with me. I don't have to face death alone. Not yet.*

The need to make contact was immediate and vital. Jenchae reached out his hand to the stranger, who stared at it as if the gesture had no meaning, then turned away, eyes darting from wall to wall.

Jenchae remembered the crushing claustrophobia of his own first moments in this squat, square chamber, five meters to a side and not quite four high, floor and walls of slick, black tiles reflecting the amber lamps above so that the room seemed covered in dusty moons.

The lights never changed; there was no chronometer, no viewscreen, no way but the meal intervals to measure the passing of time. No sound but a soft hiss of air through the ceiling pores. No furnishings but a single narrow cot set in an alcove carved out of the wall opposite the door.

To the left as he faced the cot was a small lavatory with a flimsy door, to the right an alcove half a meter on a side, which served out meals and devoured returned dishes. There had been an antiseptic scent to the room when Jenchae was first locked in. He couldn't smell it anymore. He'd adapted. Even the cell's dimensions had become correct. But in this new man's presence, the room, once again, was tiny.

A rumbling began under their feet, expanding to a deep drone as the ship lifted off. Jenchae tried to picture them rocketing skyward, but it was impossible to imagine such violence behind that soft sound. The inertial dampers deadened all sense of acceleration. His heart knocked. There was deception in moving with no sensation of moving.

Our journey into death.

He glanced at his companion, who stood still, eyes closed.

The ship underway, the drone faded. Jenchae summoned up his better self: the one who gave comfort, the good host.

"I'm Jenchae. Welcome." He spoke in Ash'torian because it was the common language, not his own and not a sverra's. It hit the ears flat, without the nuance of his native tongue.

The man smiled briefly. *"Welcome?"*

Jenchae returned the clipped smile. Welcome to my prison cell: well come indeed. He admired the sverra's Ash'torian, a delocalized Outlier accent, almost native.

"Elek." The man gave his name like an afterthought as he paced the perimeter of the room. Crossing to the lav, he knocked the door back fast as if expecting an ambush. The sudden thump, more than the action, made Jenchae flinch. Elek glanced around the lav, then turned back to his cellmate. "So tell me what's wrong with this scenario."

"In which respect?"

"A prison cell with a separate lav — with a door ideal for jumping out at unsuspecting guards."

"They'd say an Ash'torian soldier is more than equal to ambush."

Elek smirked.

"But they could always gas us if they wanted to put us down."

Elek nodded at the cot. "And only one bed? A separate lav for one prisoner? Or one bed for two?"

"It's a *za'jen*."

Elek gave an uncomprehending shake of his head.

"A 'test of honor.'" Jenchae broke the word into its root components.

"Marvelous. That's where they torture people, isn't it, to test their strength of will?"

"Only in the ancient times. In this version, people are given a set of conditions and left to themselves to sort out what they do with them."

"That's it?"

"That's it."

"That's stupid." Elek ran a hand along the wall. "They've already condemned us; what's to test?"

Jenchae shrugged. "It's designed to prepare our souls for the Quol'shab, the Death Planet."

"You believe that, do you? A special planet just for executions."

"Oh no, it's not a single planet. More a task shifted from planet to planet."

Elek's smile this time held a touch of condescension.

Leaving the old man to his fantasies. Many doubted the existence of the Death Planet. It would, of course, be more economical to execute prisoners in space while maintaining the myth of the sacred, cleansing resting grounds.

Yet that, at bottom, was Outlier thinking, the reasoning of people who subsisted amid such scarcity that efficiency must be a way of life. But Ash'tor was not a poor Nation. It was a Nation of believers, who saw necessity in the ceremonies of death for the condemned. Jenchae himself had seen it — the Quol'shab — long ago: to go there was part of the training of every lawyer schooled in Ash'tor.

But he did not want his companion to know that.

After a moment, Jenchae asked, "Were you a Striver?" Not every Outlier was an active Striver against the Ash'torian regime. Most were too busy eking out a living. Yet if Elek were a Striver, then he and Jenchae were allies.

Elek answered, "Yes, that's right," and crossing to the nearest corner, he sat down on the floor.

Jenchae did not like that answer: it was too fast and plain, like an easy lie. But he made himself smile. "That makes two." Following his companion's example, he sat down where he'd been standing.

To look at Elek made his consciousness prickle. At first, he assumed that he was picking up a telepathic impression of the other man's mind. Now, it struck him that the crackling he sensed was no more than his own emotion.

Elek himself had a quiet mind. . . a silent mind.

In Ash'tor, telepathic etiquette reserved true mind-sharing for close friends and family. Yet each Ash'torian was raised as part of the Naha'jûn, a subliminal collective that provided comfort and cohesion. When enough of its members were nearby, Jenchae, who was a strong telepath, sensed the Naha'jûn as an inaudible hum.

Elek was not of the Naha'jûn. But that only intensified the mystery: being an Outlier should make his mind louder. Among Outliers, though "closed" minds blocked the transfer of most thoughts, they still echoed emotions.

Elek's mind did not echo. It did not hum. Its silence was a vacuum.

Perhaps Elek had no telepathic center in his brain: a throwback to pre-engineered times. Jenchae had heard of such rare mutes.

He longed suddenly to touch this man's mind. He hadn't realized how thin his solitude had stretched him until given this chance of contact.

Could he touch this man? Did he dare?

After decades — in some cases centuries — of Ash'torian occupation, most Outliers, including sverra, followed a looser version of Ash'torian mind etiquette. To nudge Elek's mind might seem too forward — but not offensive, as it would to an

Ash'torian. Jenchae would knock at the door and see who answered.

He pressed outward softly, advertising his presence, requesting a response. It was passing a hand through empty air. He pressed a little harder; still nothing. Yet Elek had heard him.

"What?" he asked crossly, eyes fastening on Jenchae.

"Forgive me." Jenchae raised a placating hand. "I merely meant to invite contact."

Elek stared.

"It was rude of me."

Elek's eyes narrowed a little.

After a pause, Jenchae continued, "I was thinking that here, so near our ends, it's surely a moment for minds to meet. To find company in death."

A few seconds more, Elek said nothing, then, "Have you thought about escape?"

Jenchae's heart lurched. Escape had become too paradisiacal a fantasy. "Thought about it. Dreamed up plans, but nothing that would stand a chance of working — not really. I serve myself better by preparing for death. But if you're planning to try to escape, I'll help."

"I'm not."

Why not? Jenchae didn't ask. *I did offend him by my mind touch.* He would have to step back and begin again. "You must have been an influential Striver."

Elek's eyes narrowed. "Why?"

"Well, formal execution's usually reserved for leaders."

Elek crossed his arms. "Then you must have been influential."

There was an invitation in those words that Jenchae could not resist.

"I've been a Striver for decades, most recently guiding peaceful protesters on Taenquûn. To give Ash'tor their due, they left us alone at the start. But when we began to impact the ore sales, they began the arrests." His mind ran off faces — so young, those Taenquûnian miners torn from their friends, death's irredressability etched across straining mouths. He studied his fingers. "I wrote a letter of protest to the Nine Ministries —"

A snicker burst from Elek. "How many years did you say you'd been a Striver?"

Jenchae sighed. "Every once in a while, it behooves us to remember that hope is not the same thing as idiocy. No, I did not expect the Ministries to listen. But is that a reason to stop talking?"

"What did they do?"

"They picked me up."

Those last minutes were as vivid as life: diving into the hiding closet at the sound of the soldiers forcing the door, an Ash'torian voice: "Where is Denned Jenchae?"

And her, Fenen, his friend, the local resistance leader, shouting indignantly, "How dare you come barging into my house."

Scuffling sounds, a squeak. "Your daughter or Denned. The choice is yours."

"You have no right —"

Jenchae did not wait for Fenen to finish. He surged out of the closet, sick at the depths to which his cowardice had brought him, risking that child's life. And reeling, he realized he'd implicated them by his very surrender.

"She didn't know I was here," he said, fabricating as he talked. "An acquaintance — mine, not theirs. . . a repairman who serviced this house, told me there was a cellar I could hide in."

As the soldiers dragged him out, his friends' eyes haunted him. The Ash'torians wouldn't believe him. They never believed in innocence.

His legs were stiff. Thankful for the distraction, he concentrated on stretching them. "I was hoping for a showy trial," he told Elek. "I thought it might generate positive publicity. But they tried me in the basement, as they say." He shrugged. "Here I am."

"A martyr."

Jenchae considered. "Well, to those who know what happened maybe. Not many."

Elek smiled.

"And you?" Jenchae pursued.

The sverra's face went blank. "I was an infiltrator for a Striver group. But I was sent here on charges of murder."

Murder.

Plain murder. Not political.

"Were the charges true?"

"I'd assure you that you're safe with me, but I'm a little tired of lying."

Jenchae tensed, processing this statement. It had none of the intonation of a threat: simply a fact. A fact stated too flatly. It sounded like a lie, a careless lie never intended to be taken for truth. Or a speech, rehearsed perhaps — but not untrue? "Who did you kill?"

"I don't know. Very many people."

"How?"

"Fast." Elek laughed. The sharp noise twisted Jenchae's gut. "So take that as some consolation. They didn't suffer much."

Jenchae wrestled his voice calm. "So you're planning to kill me?"

All at once, Elek was sober. "You're about to die anyway. Do you care?"

"I find I do."

A silence. "No, I'm not *planning* to."

Jenchae tried to find comfort in that.

But what was this man? Which way would he dart? Was he even a murderer at all, or just demented — or lying? Demented liar? Murderer? Striver?

"Why have you killed others, then?"

Elek's eyes bored into Jenchae's; then he grinned with a child's sincerity. "I don't know. I've killed people since I was a boy."

Jenchae peered at Elek through the twilight of the cell. His white face was lined around the eyes and mouth, hair graying at the temples.

"How old are you?" A tremor crept into Jenchae's voice.

Elek sighed. "Two hundred and sixty. . . three," he answered, as if adding it up as he went.

A laugh escaped from Jenchae: "Sverra genes! And here's me: a hundred and twenty and not nearly so well preserved."

Elek made no reply but to smile with a palpable absence of amusement. That smile silenced Jenchae.

~•~

Some time later, Jenchae was startled by a clang. Even as his head jerked toward the sound, he realized it was their meal, the second of the day. Two bowls of rice and two water cups, ceramoid dishware red as maple leaves in autumn. Their clanging was nothing like the clink of just his own bowl and cup.

Jenchae handed Elek his food, and the two sat a little apart.

Elek picked his spoon out of his bowl. "How long have you been here?"

"Ten days, counting two meals to a day."

"How do you know that's a day?"

Jenchae didn't know for certain, of course. "It feels like it. It felt that way to my belly when I first came here."

"How do you know they don't change the intervals between meals?"

Jenchae shrugged. "They have no reason to."

"Spite," Elek suggested.

"No. The Ash'torians design these last days to help us let go of this universe. That cause is best served by physical regularity, not mind-games."

"You seem to know a lot about it."

That Jenchae did not answer.

Elek took a bite of rice and glanced around the room. "That server —" he nodded at the little alcove. "You return the dishes to it?"

Jenchae nodded.

"Have you tried keeping the dishes?"

"I did at first. I kept the cup so I could get water from the lav sink when I wanted it. . . and because I liked the splash of color in the room."

"And?"

"They stopped sending a water cup. The water they send tastes cleaner, cooler than the lav water."

Jenchae liked Elek's questions; they were practical, not the questions of a madman. But that didn't mean the madman was gone. And if Elek attacked him, the guards would not save him. The world inside the cell was not to be interfered with.

Foolish, perhaps, for the condemned to fear murder; still, Jenchae would not bow to this new, violent death. Life remained precious, in its final moments most of all.

He kept his mind open for unblocked mental impulses. That, at least, could not be impolite: just to be alert to thoughts left accessible. Such impressions couldn't give him open truth, but they would hint at it. Still Elek was silent — and the silence was beginning to beat on Jenchae.

I'm not seeing this the right way. It doesn't matter if his story is the truth. If he's lying, that lie conveys his truth. At bottom, the truth is all any of us speaks. So believe — and reach deeper.

"Have you ever had life-modification training?"

Elek glanced up sharply. "Many times. It hasn't worked."

"Not in Ash'tor, was it?"

"No, not likely I'd end up a patient in Ash'tor."

Jenchae straightened his back and shifted his legs, wishing the floor was not so hard. Done with his meal, he set his bowl aside.

"Did they give you drugs?"

"Sometimes."

Jenchae leaned his palms back on the floor. "And the drugs didn't work, you say?"

"They tranqued me out. It would stop the rage all right; they'd let me go. But I didn't stay on them."

Jenchae was reassured by Elek's willingness to talk.

"Did the drugs change your mind too much?"

Elek hesitated. "They made me too groggy to work, and when I couldn't work, I couldn't afford them."

Jenchae shook his head. "Ash'torian medicine would have done better for you."

"It was Ash'torian — cheap, Outlier hand-down Ash'torian meds."

Jenchae nodded, realizing with relief that the simple act of talking had dampened his fear of Elek. "It's hard to feel compelled to harm people."

"I don't see how it matters now." Elek resumed eating, speaking between mouthfuls. "The only person I could harm now is you. Soon I'll be dead, and you'll be dead, and that will be that. So why should I care?"

You first, and me second. That's interesting. Jenchae shrugged. "Peace."

"Peace," Elek repeated the word and laughed.

"Certainly." Jenchae kept his face its most sincere.

Elek set aside his plate. "You think I'm not at peace? You think I hate myself for what I've done?" He grinned. "When I remember what it's like to crush the life out of a living being, all I can think of is how wonderful it feels. That's when I know peace."

It's the truth. Jenchae's doubt melted. And still, he was not afraid. No, that was wrong: he was — but afraid of forces more powerful than Elek. Elek had stirred the pool, bringing heavy, old things back into the light. *I've been here before.* With Akhté: the man's copper face flashed before him. *This is truth, and I owe him the truth in return.* "I've felt elation when I've killed too, but elation isn't peace. No, I don't believe you feel peace."

Elek studied him. "I thought you were a nonviolent protester."

"Not then, when Ash'tor had just killed my mother; I had no wish for peace."

"What changed?"

Yes, he had been here before. He had spoken while Akhté had refused to understand — or understood too well perhaps. "I came to remember my mother's life: how her contentment had come from within, through the. . . inability of the outer world to command hope or despair. She knew her life had been good because she'd made it so. I took that into my heart and sought peace."

"How old were you?"

"When I made that resolution? Forty-six."

"I'm a bit older than that."

"You're young for a sverra."

Jenchae ached to see who this man was, to make him knowable and let the knowing quell the fear. "You could allow me to touch your mind. Then, perhaps, I could help you."

Elek fixed him with unreadable eyes. "I can't."

CHAPTER TWO

> Only twice did I turn in one of my own. One was
> a mistake. The other was Elek Onx: I had no
> qualms about turning him in.

Memoirs of Fahnor Naquel, 2139 A.E.

Mad gods, thought Elek, *the man is annoying!* So why did Elek keep talking to him? The answer dawned unexpected and obvious: he talked to him because he enjoyed telling the truth. He hadn't realized till now how heavy the lies had become.

~ • ~

For a while, Elek had done all right with Naquel's Strivers, volunteered for the jobs that gave him a chance to kill a lot of Rapts*. That felt good. But gradually, it ceased to be enough. Perhaps the violence bred violence. Perhaps the zeal of Naquel's revolutionaries flamed him. It didn't matter. For whatever reason, the rage grew harder to suppress. And then that boy, Neeja, made that stupid slip, told that spy where they were heading. And they'd almost been captured, and something in Neeja's insipid gray eyes had been too much for Elek, and he snapped the boy's neck. He managed to blame it on one of the Rapts, but Urno was suspicious. And since he didn't want to have to kill her for that, he embroidered his story to lay her distrust to rest.

Yet she confronted him.

---

*"Rapt" is a pejorative term for an Ash'torian. It stands for "enraptured ones," a play on Ash'torian religiosity.

Translator's Note

"You think I don't know what you are. I know. You're a reptile. You're a subhuman who sees humans as things you can break like toys. You have no business striving with Naquel."

It had been a long time since anyone had called Elek subhuman. Trals* were stronger than humans, after all, so most humans were wisely wary of antagonizing them.

But here was Urno mounting insult on insult. Suddenly, he was so sick of her face that he hit her, pleased to watch her crumple on the floor. A moment later, the whole thing struck him as inevitable and wearying.

Then Naquel stormed in; Elek hadn't known, of course, that Urno had set him watching. Naquel yelled, and others came and tranqued Elek down, though he tore some tendons in Naquel's shoulder before he lost consciousness.

He hadn't wanted to do that. He liked Naquel — Naquel, who had pulled him out of the desert and got him to half-believe again that he could live with other people.

By the time he wrenched Naquel's shoulder, he was a little surprised he was still struggling. He'd already known it was all over, and the ending was almost a relief.

"You have no business striving with Naquel."

When the others who had prodded him into the holding cell left, Naquel sat before him on the other side of the sizzling force field.

"There is a place for mercy," he said, brown eyes blazing. "But *they* have to understand that people like you are not Strivers. You are not one of us; you're a common killer. I disavow you. I leave you to them. I want *them* to know how deeply you disgust me."

And he got up and walked away, the door swishing shut behind him.

~ • ~

---

* "Tral" is the Manyrock sverras' word for their species. It derives from the standard Keshnul word for the species, "*tralorváti*," which translates as "strong bioengineered humans."

Author's Note

After Elek and Jenchae had eaten, they returned their dishes to the wall box, which whisked them away like a transit tunnel taking tourists on vacation. As soon as they vanished, Elek missed the cups and bowls, the red and orange gone free, leaving him locked in this black-on-black cell.

He sat in the corner to the right of the door because it felt safest, even though he knew he was not the one most immediately in danger.

He did not like Jenchae and wondered if he'd kill him. He had said the killing made him happy, which was true, in a way, sometimes. . . but not here. Not in this cell.

Yet there was nothing he could do about it.

Jenchae was still sitting in the middle of the room, about two meters away. Too close. The cell seemed to radiate from him. Jenchae's eyes were closed, face pointed forward.

Meditating, Elek thought. He wondered, not for the first time, what meditation must be like. The nearest he could imagine was being almost asleep: that state you're only aware of when startled back to wakefulness. But he'd heard that meditation did things to calm the spirit that sleep did not.

Elek studied Jenchae as if he could peer into the pathways of his brain. He didn't reach out his mind; he couldn't, hadn't in more years than he could count. He just watched. Jenchae had said he was — what? — a hundred and twenty? He looked older. His face was furrowed so deeply that Elek could see the lines clearly in the twilight, even against the dark brown of Jenchae's skin. Everything about Jenchae was dark except his hair: dark skin in dark coveralls — dark eyes too, when they were open. His short hair, which Elek presumed was gray, glinted gingery in the orange lamps. If Elek blurred his eyes a little, he could make Jenchae disappear into the darkness, except for that dull, orangey hair, like a moon that casts a bleary glow through fog when all you want is blackness.

Blackness did away with hard edges and vindicated Elek's right to sleep. He liked blackness within sleep as well, awaking to remember nothing, not even a ghost of a dream. He hoped that death would be that way.

Dreams were almost always bad. And rare now, fortunately.

Elek thought about Jenchae's probing fingers in his mind. Like a doctor asking questions about his childhood. Like a child poking at a dying lizard. When Elek saw someone do that, sometimes he would grab a rock and smash the lizard, and he would tell the child it was because he was a sverra and his ancestors had come from the Kiri worlds, where it was common decency to put a dying thing out of its misery. Sometimes he wondered if he was telling the truth.

That prodding sort of person irritated him. How could such a man become a leader of Strivers? Who'd put up with him?

But Jenchae had spoken of the killing as if he'd understood, at least a little. And there he was, meditating. Being at peace? What must that be like? Like the calm after killing but without the killing?

Jenchae had seemed willing to show Elek that peace. He had reached Elek's mind. No one had done that in decades. It was worrying, exposing. Yet if this man was that strong and could get in that close, was it possible he was the very person to quiet Elek's fury? Elek would like that. It was hard when the rage came and there was nothing he could do. It was worse when he tried to resist it, which he almost always had to, if he didn't want to end up being thrown in a prison.

Prison. He smiled at the irony. Most times, resisting worked — but it failed just often enough. And when the full shriek of the rage came on him, he was never able to crush it. Someone else might beat him down, as they had to save Urno, but over himself, he was powerless — powerless and free. To resist: that was excruciating, like trying to stop an orgasm. Prison seemed better. A short journey now, and he would never have to resist again.

But he didn't want to kill Jenchae. All at once, he felt old and strained and wanted to sleep. Recently, he'd started to picture himself just clinging to an outcropping of rock in the face of a sandstorm, expecting every moment to be torn into the wind. And the wind was in him, and if it didn't die soon, it would tear him to shreds. He wondered if Jenchae could make the wind die — just for these last days.

~•~

Too sultry in this cell. Elek tried to convince himself that the air only seemed to be sticky.

After a time, he missed Jenchae's prattle. At least, it was a distraction. He wondered how much longer they had before they died, wondered how much longer till Jenchae spoke again. Good bet the chatter would come first. And sure enough, perhaps an hour after eating: "Would you like to sleep on the cot tonight?"

"Night?" The orange lamps on the ceiling had not dimmed.

"After each two meals, I think of it as night. Breakfast and supper and night and morning."

"You're offering to sleep on the floor?" Elek didn't like that; as a ploy to win his gratitude, it wasn't very subtle.

Jenchae scratched his neck thoughtfully. "In honor of your first day here."

Elek eyed him with undisguised suspicion. "But you're an old human. I can hear your joints creak. You know you should have the bed."

Jenchae smiled tightly. "You're very thoughtful," *for a murderer*, Elek finished the thought to himself.

"And you're —" Elek stopped. He couldn't see what he'd accomplish by challenging Jenchae, and he certainly wasn't going to pretend to be taken in by him. He knew that Jenchae was trying to win his trust so he could poke around in his head.

But even without trust, it might be worth it. Might.

Carefully, he asked, "Did you miss it. . . the elation?"

Jenchae blinked, then seemed to understand. "Of killing, you mean? Yes, I did. But not enough to return to it."

"Then you can't help me."

Jenchae stared at him with obsidian eyes. Elek stared back, refusing to be cowed, until Jenchae looked down and got stiffly to his feet. He ambled to the bed alcove and, maneuvering around its low ceiling, lay down on his side, still facing Elek.

For a second, Elek was relieved to have him gone from the center of the room. Then, all at once, Jenchae seemed a predator in a cave. His move to the bed had looked too calculated; Elek wasn't sure what to make of it.

"Why?" said Jenchae.

"Why what?"

"Why are you so sure I can't help you?"

"Why are you so eager to?"

Jenchae rested his head under his arm. "Fair enough. It's what I do. It's what I've dedicated my life to, helping people."

That came close to being the most ridiculous thing Elek had ever heard: *I want to help you because I want to help*? Couldn't the man think up a more plausible lie than that?

"And what do I do for you? What's the price?"

Jenchae sighed. "I understand," he said with air of disappointment. "Who believes in good will these days? Say I'm bored then. It's true. Say that you'll take my mind off my impending death. You are." He paused. "Say I want to keep you from killing me."

Obviously. How had Elek managed to miss that? But just what was he planning to do to Elek in order to keep him from killing. Help? Would it *help*?

"Honestly," said Jenchae, "what do you have to lose?"

What did he have to lose? Not much. His sanity at worst perhaps if the man did something vicious to his mind, gave him visions or voices. But sometimes his sanity seemed tenuous in any case. And if he did go mad, he wouldn't live to endure it long.

But odds were it was all moot. This man couldn't help him. Jenchae might think he knew something about killing. He didn't know.

Elek spoke his mind: "The way you describe it, killing and not being tempted back to it: it's not like that for me. Never has been." He'd been planning to say more but found he couldn't.

Jenchae's eyes glinted from the shadow of the alcove. "Everyone is different." Elek endeavored not to sneer. "I don't mean to imply that I understand you. That would be absurd. But I knew a man once who you remind me of. He had. . . difficulty controlling his impulses too. I tried to help him."

The "tried" told Elek all he needed to know. But just to see what Jenchae would say, he asked, "Did you succeed?"

Jenchae lay still for some moments. Elek thought he could see the wrinkled face twitch in the gloom. "Let's say I got the sand out of one shoe."

Elek did not like that either: using expressions from the Tral homeworld. Another attempt to win him over. Anger tingled in his throat, dogged by a twinge of fear. If the rage came now. . . But it was nothing yet; he could swallow it down. He made his hands go limp in his lap and watched Jenchae until calm returned.

"So," Elek said, "you partly helped him. What part?"

"I helped him. . . for a while." He hesitated. "Akhté was a hypertelepath, you know?"

"He had a lot of mind pain?" Elek didn't know much about hypertelepathy, but he knew that hypertelepaths had trouble blocking out people's thoughts; for some, it was supposedly excruciating.

"When I met him," Jenchae went on, "he was working with a resistance cell in the Leddie-Sama Block. Violent work. Full-out war on Ash'tor; you know the sort of thing."

"Then he must have had a lot of mind pain. I'd think he'd have fled from violence. Or did he like being in pain?"

Jenchae hesitated. "Did he like being in pain? Yes, to an extent, he did. But he hated Ash'tor, and he had a belief in his moral responsibility to see his enemies dead."

Expressions like "moral responsibility" had a quaint ring in Elek's ears. He smiled. "Was he religious?"

To Elek's discomfort, Jenchae smiled back. "Well, he was, but not, I think, in the way you mean. His sense of responsibility didn't come from religion."

He paused, plainly waiting for Elek to ask what it came from.

Elek fed him silence till Jenchae went on, "He'd had problems with his family." (*Who hasn't?* thought Elek.) "His father was a hypertelepath who went insane, you see. Hurt his family — in those special ways a hypertelepath can. From that, Akhté derived his doctrine: kill your enemies when you have the chance."

"That's not moral; that's practical." To himself, Elek thought, *To kill is not insanity.*

Jenchae's face, from the bed, had an odd, sideways look. "For him, it was moral. There was very little practical in how Akhté lived. He accustomed himself to feeling people die around him. He'd had some training — a lot actually — to control the bombardment of others' thoughts —" Jenchae shook his head "— but it broke down."

"Did he 'crumble'?" That happened to some HTs; they went mad. That was probably what had happened to the man's father.

"No," said Jenchae quickly, then, "well, maybe at the very end. He had a bad experience."

Elek raised an eyebrow.

"But he was killed before it could seriously damage his mind."

I don't like the way this is turning.

Jenchae was frowning. "By the time I met him, his sense of his duty to kill Ash'torians had given him a predilection for violent action. It caused him mind pain, but I believe it had become an outlet for it too. I provided a different outlet: the release that comes from calm, from rest."

"From 'peace'?" Elek watched him closely.

"Of a sort," Jenchae leaned forward. "I suspect that you have a kind of mind pain too. Why else the violence? I'd like to help you overcome it. Even if it only works for a time. That's all we'll need."

He failed his Akhté and he wants to make up for it with me. That much didn't take a hypertelepath to see.

Still, if it worked . . . If.

"Enjoy the bed," said Elek and lay down on the tiles.

CHAPTER THREE

Every one of the Outlying Planets once belonged
to the Sama Empire. Every one once glistened
with the tech, the art, the philosophy, the human
community of the Samas. At the End of the Kiri-
Sama War, these worlds were devastated, left for
dead. The few Samas who survived attempted to
recolonize them, but the center of Sama culture
was gone, and for the populations that came later,
simply surviving was struggle enough. But now,
my kinfolk, there is a new center. It is Ash'tor. It
is the Naha'jûn.

Public Address by the Naha'jé Ba'lahr Y-Quo'dem Do'sé
(2004 A.E.)

The yad raised his gun.

But in Jenchae's dream, the yad was Akhté, bathed in the
sunset. And though Jenchae curled small and still behind his
mother's loom, the fiery man had found him. The gun seemed a
black tunnel projecting from Akhté's face as he said, "Jenchae,
you make me love you as a planet loves the sun." But his voice
was Elek's.

~•~

Jenchae awoke on the cot to a sick churning of the blood.
He did not want to be the sun Elek orbited. All he wanted was
to find a commonality of soul.

To reach Elek might be the last meaningful thing Jenchae
ever did. If he could see the man's mind, if he could understand
what drove Elek's anger, he could help him to come to terms
with it.

But like a suicide, Elek refused solutions.

So silence filled the cell like water to drown in.

In this black room, the door alone was gray, not tiled, reflecting no lamps, a portal taunting Jenchae with the illusion of escape.

Elek was curled asleep in the corner, face and hands luminous against his dark coverall.

Jenchae yearned to have his cell to himself. He didn't crave solitude; that wasn't it. It was that man, that murderer, that implacable, inaccessible, self-defeatist silent mind. Let him keep his silence. Jenchae wanted him gone!

Several slow breaths calmed him.

However I long to recoil, I mustn't despise him. Even through the silence, I can try to do him good. (Do better than I did with —)

He struggled out of the low cot alcove.

A chair, my jailers, would not come amiss. You realize there's an old man with arthritis here?

If Ash'tor absorbed the Outlying Planets, everyone could get meds. People like me would be cured in one treatment. That's what they say. And they'd do it — in their way.

The bitterness rose.

Yes, they'd do it — and tyrannize our industries, our religions, our art, Elek's world, my world. Was it the dream that set his mind on his mother? He could almost see the wicker-weaving leaning on her wall, brown and gold reeds chasing round like pond ripples.

~ • ~

"It's attractive, but it has no spirit," Ase'qem had said, a dark, stick-thin figure gazing cross-armed at the tapestry. Stout and bright, his mother laughed. For a moment, Jenchae hated her for that.

He had last seen Ase'qem two years before, when he was twelve. He had not liked her then. This time, his heart had fallen when his mother greeted her at the door. And rather than come forth to meet her, he stood in the doorway of the common room unseen, eyes fixed on the discord of her blue army uniform against the warmth of his mother's weaving. He watched her claim their rooms as a spider bends blades of grass into its web.

"I can find you a real job though." Ase'qem wasn't even looking at the weaving. "I have it from one of the Clan

Guardians that there will be a new annual festival here in honor of Tamehe'lem, the Messenger of God." She made a brief obeisance with her hand. "They'll want fine tapestries. Important, religious work. You can make yourself a name."

"Could you put my name in with the Clan Guardian, perhaps?" his mother asked in thickly accented Ash'torian.

"Of course," Ase'qem's smile flashed white in her ebony face. "There's no one else even whispered for the job yet."

Jenchae balled his hands into fists. "Don't grovel to them like that, Shoten!" he barked in his own language. "What do you want to be slaving over their gods for?"

Before his mother could speak, Ase'qem, scowling, chastised him in Ash'torian: "Jen'chae. That is no fit way to speak to your birth mother or to greet me after my absence." To his mother, she said, "Could I have heard him right, calling Tamehe'lem a god? You should teach him better."

His mother met the Ash'torian's gaze. "I have taught him well, Ase'qem. He knows Tamehe'lem is a Clan Founder,* of course. He was speaking of the gods to mean your whole religion."

"He should speak more respectfully of religion."

"Yes, in that, I agree." Shoten fixed a firm, blue eye on Jenchae.

"But, Shoten, *she* doesn't —"

Ase'qem interrupted: "He should speak more respectfully to you, as well. How is it, Jen'chae, that you call your own mother by her given name as if she were a cousin?"

"That is not disrespect," Shoten put in. "That is our people's way."

---

* The Clan Founders are historical figures who have attained the status of legends in Ash'tor. At one time, all Ash'torians belonged to one of the Nine Clans. Today, many families still claim Clan affiliation. The nine Clan Founders are Ahma'hé, Qhe'byq, Sham'taht, Yor, Sorq, Tamehe'lem, Do'shé, En'zah, and Abte'nyq.

Translator's Note

"I know it is your way. But it marks you as barbaric. And you, Shoten, I had always thought to be more civilized!"

Jenchae lunged forward. "How is it you dare speak to her like that?" he shouted in Ash'torian.

"You — " Ase'qem stopped. She glanced at Shoten, who raised an eyebrow at her in a secret way from which Jenchae was excluded. "You come to her defense at least. That is the mark of a good son."

Shoten put her arm around him.

"Welcome back to Yorûn, beloved," she said to Ase'qem.

~•~

Poor Ase'qem. Jenchae could say that now, with so many decades' distance. She had tried but never understood.

Melancholy followed him into the lav and out again. When he returned, Elek was blinking sleepily, twisting kinks out of his neck. The man's very living presence unnerved Jenchae.

Yet Jenchae's mother had looked with charity on everyone. She'd even liked Ase'qem; she'd loved her. For Shoten, Jenchae could embrace Elek in spirit, even without mind-speech. Without speech at all.

He concentrated on stretching.

Elek rose and walked past him to the lav. When he returned, he stood, arms folded, and watched Jenchae with a slight smile. Jenchae was surprised by how much that expression warmed him. It bespoke proportion.

Elek said, "There really is nothing to do here, is there?"

Jenchae swallowed down a philosophical answer. "Not much."

Elek's smile broadened. "You're less irritating today."

"You seem about the same." Immediately, Jenchae regretted the words. A vole caged with a cat must be polite. He lowered himself to the ground for floor exercises.

Elek watched for a minute or so, then said, "Is it really just one day since we left the port?"

"One day. Maybe our last." Jenchae sighed. "I wonder how many of my friends from Taenquûn are here on this ship."

"Can you sense any?"

"No. Outside this cell, I sense an undercurrent of distress. I feel the Naha'jûn humming. But no individual people." He smiled slightly. "Not even you, for that matter."

Elek eyed him hard. "It makes you lonely."

That comment was more incisive than Jenchae had expected. He wasn't sure how to respond. "Less lonely than before you came."

At breakfast, Jenchae kept quiet. But inside he was nurturing a sense of camaraderie. He and Elek *were* both Outliers, after all. Both were here by the grace of Ash'tor. (He cut off a flash of the gun rising.)

How could this man be a murderer? What outrage had bent his spirit on retribution?

The silence hurt. Jenchae didn't care what twistedness lay in Elek's mind. It would be better than nothingness. But Elek had refused to share himself, and that was Elek's choice.

"You know," said Jenchae, "I may have been wrong to suggest we touch minds."

Elek glanced at him sharply. "Why?"

"Well, it's plain it — it doesn't seem a good idea to you, and I certainly don't want to push it on you."

Elek's gaze was intent. "I thought I said I'd think about it."

A wave of vertigo swept through Jenchae. "You did? I thought —"

"I just don't like to be bludgeoned."

"Of course. Well, as you will. Perhaps just by talking —"

"Do you come from Taenquûn?"

"I — Yorûn." Just a coincidence that Elek asked about his origins the very morning (morning!) that his mind was lost in them? Or was something in their thoughts already joined? Or something that transcended telepathy?

Elek nodded. "Ah, yes, the warring sister worlds."

"No, no. Yorûn and Hahûn haven't warred for a long time."

~ • ~

"Just look at how the two planets fight," Ase'qem had said later that same visit. "If Ash'tor weren't here, Yor'ûn and Ha'hûn would still be flinging missiles at each other."

"It's not your concern either way," Jenchae said. "It's our problem to manage without you."

"Of course it's our concern when people are slaughtering each other to no purpose but hate. Tra'hae calls all people to care for one another."

"But your people slaughter us!" Jenchae was squirming in his chair, wishing by every god in the stars that his mother had not insisted he sit down and "catch up" with this pulp-grinding Rapt.

Ase'qem grew still. "Jen'chae, I know that Shoten's people have suffered at Ash'tor's hands. I know that our ways are not yours, and that you are attached to your beliefs. And some of your customs are good, and, yes, perhaps some good ones will be lost."

"So basically, you admit —"

"Do not interrupt your elder kin." Her voice was strangely mild. "I admit that no great change can be brought about without sacrifice. Such is the wisdom of Tra'hae. But I will tell you a thing about your loss: it is inevitable. This is so because enough people will yearn for Ash'torian ways that, little by little, your people will embrace them."

"You're completely brain-warped."

"It has happened, Jen'chae. In the N-Block worlds, the *Naha'jûn* Block. Many of them were once as Yor'ûn is, but now they are proud people of the Naha'jûn. Yor'ûn will follow. The Yor'ûnians want peace and prosperity and will see that *we* can give it."

"You have nothing we could want."

"We have art. We have superior technology. We understand how to live within our ecological means. We control population growth better than you do. We are not prey to the same superstitions. We have cohesion, strength, stability, love of family and Nation, of the spirit, of God. We will bring you to our ways because deep down, we know our center."

~•~

We are conquered peoples, and that unites us.

That was their common outrage and their common need — not to fall to that rage, *not to hold Ash'tor in contempt as they hold us, not to become like them.*

"It isn't that bad on Yorûn," Jenchae asserted, as much for himself as Elek. "Ash'torian occupation united Yorûn and Hahûn against a common foe. And Ash'tor brought Yorûn a measure of prosperity, so there's less desperation and violence than in a lot of places."

"They say the same thing about Manyrock." The sverra homeworld.

"You disagree," Jenchae prompted, eager to hear Elek speak of himself. It must have hurt sverra pride to be conquered by a physically weaker race. After all, the Ash'torian conquest of Yorûn had shamed the Samas, and they, at least, were the same species.

Elek hesitated. "I really haven't been back to Manyrock in years — decades."

"I haven't been to Yorûn in decades either." More than a century since he'd splashed through the fields in the big dome, the fans buzzing, the reeds crimson, saffron, magenta — each with its weaving name.

You're away and it changes. I'd describe Yorûn like starlight from forty light-years away. I look up and see a nova, but it's already over. And so, too, is Elek's Manyrock.

"I don't know why the Samas wanted to colonize Manyrock anyway," said Elek suddenly. "After the War, it was almost all deep desert, not exactly conducive to human life. They were asking for a slip-slide of trouble."

"They fought with the sverra a long time, didn't they, the Manyrock Samas?"

"That was inevitable, wasn't it? If you're thirsty enough, you fight for water, and it's not as if the Sama colonists could pull water out of stones."

"My mother thought the same thing."

"About Manyrock?" Surprise in Elek's voice.

"About colonizing rough worlds, that it's hardly worth it." He laughed lightly. "You see, with or without reading minds, we still have things in common."

Elek gave an uncertain half-smile. "We'll see."

But Jenchae's thoughts were flowing back to his mother.

~•~

"Well, you two know what I think," Shoten had said in her imperfect Ash'torian. "I think the Samas should have made a functional biosphere on these worlds before to recolonize them. Who wants to live by the pleasure of an atmosphere generator?"

She passed the dinner pilaf to Ase'qem, who answered, "That is a point, but one must admire the drive of people who carve life out of a desert still redolent with death."

Did she just praise my people? Jenchae wondered. He wanted to ask her, but he could not quite bow low enough. She might be family, but she was still the enemy.

~•~

Jenchae glanced up to see Elek watching him.

Is that how he feels for his Sama side? Does he see them, as I see Ash'tor, as the ravagers? "So were the sverra and Samas still fighting when you were a boy?"

Elek didn't answer at once. "They weren't playing boulder tag."

That's how they do it. They embroil us in their hatred until it becomes ours too.

~•~

Shoten had shut the door and said, "The atmo-gen's on the blink again. Can you believe this mugginess? Jenchae, just look at my hair." She flipped off her hat and dabbed at the sides of her head.

At sixteen, Jenchae was a factory worker. He had gotten home a few minutes before and was sitting with a cup of ice water, flexing fingers sore from twelve hours of hand-decorating flutes. He looked up when Shoten came in and laughed. "It's gone stringy."

His mother was staring into the wall mirror. "It looks all reedy." She turned to him. "Well, they say that if you weave long enough you turn into your weaving."

Jenchae laughed harder. "Best be extra canny, you, or one day you'll wake up as one of your pictures."

"I will be Tamehe'lem," Shoten said, her arm sweeping out an exaggerated obeisance.

Jenchae folded his arms. "Here I thought it was your wise-chatter never to disrespect religion."

Shoten flopped down in the chair beside him. "Oh, Jenchae, it is not Tamehe'lem I'm mocking."

Two hours later, the gun was rising.

"You must have the wrong person," Shoten had said. But to them, the very shaking of her voice was incriminating. "I'm a wicker weaver, not a political. I'm trying just to get a living — for my son."

Jenchae stood beside her in short-cut leggings, sweating like a sprinter.

"Search the rooms," the ba'nad said to one of the yads under her command.

The pamphlets[*] were wedged between two tapestries black and orange as fire, for the festival of Tamehe'lem.

"They were given me just on the street," said Shoten.

The ba'nad said something about her having to die, that it was war — or like in a war. Jenchae would never remember clearly, for just then, his mother began to talk over them.

"Listen." She gestured at Jenchae again. "Send you a message to Ase'qem Abte'nyq that you have this youth, Denned Jenchae. He is a relative. He has citizen rights." In their own tongue, she added, "Jenchae, every place they send you, every chance you get, you tell them you belong with Ase'qem."

Za Ase'qem zacrusd. For the rest of his life it would dog him that those were her last words: you belong with Ase'qem.

With aching slowness, the gun was rising.

Then, quicker than thought, the yad fired.

---

[*] Some non-Ash'torians have expressed puzzlement at the prevalence of print documents as sources of news and commentary. The Strivers favored print sources as less likely to disclose sensitive information, such as a person's location or physical appearance, than vids, holograms, and other visual media. For some of the same reasons, the Ash'torians had already long maintained a taboo against the public circulation of visual representations for non-artistic purposes.

Translator's Note

A high-pitched hum and the violent crash of his mother thumping on the floor — and thumping and thumping as her limbs had thrashed.

They said that the neural shock knocked you out at once. The rest was just an autonomic reaction.

~ • ~

"We will bring you to our ways," she'd said, "because deep down, we know our center."

~ • ~

Jenchae bit back a surge of bile.

Why is everything reduced to one? One way, one center, one people dictating the fate of Yorûn, of Manyrock. Is there not in the whole universe enough space for more than one?

Or would the battle to be the *one* go on twisting children into murderers? *Humans fight sverra. Ash'torians fight Outliers. Compassion freezes in our veins. We are the same in this, he and I. We could reinvent compassion in one another. We must.*

But that was not enough to break the hate.

Friends, enemies: we must all come to understand each other's suffering.

Motionless, Elek was still studying Jenchae.

He'd wondered why the Samas had come to Manyrock to struggle in the desert and fight with the sverra. That should be answerable. "Times were hard for the Samas who survived the War's End. Almost all the Sama planets were ecologically wrecked —"

"Thank you for the history lesson," said Elek drily.

"But Manyrock made a phenomenal recovery —"

"Thanks to sverra eco-engineering."

"Truly? It was a monumental feat. And you must see how attractive that made the planet for Sama refugees who'd spent generations in biodomes like insects under glass."

"What is your point?"

"They had no sense of belonging to a planet. On Manyrock, they had a chance to forge a new people, a Manyrock people. And, yes, they must have guessed they'd face resistance but chosen the risk. They went there to build themselves."

To carve life in the desert.

Ase'qem had been right about that. If she had been wrong about everything else, that, at least, she had understood.

Elek was silent, staring at the ground, grappling perhaps with a Sama perspective he'd been drilled all his life to dimiss.

Jenchae continued, "Perhaps I have no right to conjecture about them. But we have to try, don't we, to interpret the experience of strangers? How else will we ever meet as comrades? I've detested Ash'tor all my life, but I must believe it has done me good to try — however imperfectly — to understand the mind of the Ash'torian."

"Did anyone ever mistake you for one?"

The words hit Jenchae like a fist in the jaw. What had prompted that? He couldn't find his voice to ask.

The silence lay thick as a night too hot for sleep.

Then, Elek said low, "I *am* part human. I am part Sama. Couldn't you tell?"

The heat rose in Jenchae's face. "Of course. Forgive me. I just — I assumed you'd define yourself as a sverra because they're rarer than humans."

"I see. Like you define yourself as human because humans are so damn rare."

"Plainly, it was a blunder."

"You're kind of an idiot, you know that?" Elek's voice was calm, at least. Annoyance, but nothing like murderous rage.

Jenchae nodded. "Apparently."

"You guessed one thing right though. I won't have you in my mind. You've made up my mind for me on that — so to speak."

"I understand."

"I sincerely doubt it."

Jenchae gasped a low, sad laugh. Yes, he'd erred in presuming that he comprehended the man. It was just what Ase'qem would do. Yes, it was Ash'torian.

For some time, he could do nothing more than bow his head and absorb that truth.

No wonder Elek distrusted him.

But without trust, no bridge could span the gulf between them. As long as Jenchae did not understand Elek, he could not help him. Yet the truest means of understanding — the union of

mind to mind — was a thing Elek would not — should not —
give to a man so stained by presumption.

He's right to refuse me. Even if he showed me his thoughts, I fear I would see myself, not him.

CHAPTER FOUR

God speaks. In gales that sandblast the writing
from temples, in continents rent plate from plate,
in suns devouring their planet-children is the
speech of God. It were better to live in times of
silence.

Mysteries of Tra'hae (c. 20th century B.E.)

When Jenchae began to prattle about Manyrock, Elek
wanted to strike him. Telling him the history of his own planet,
his own people! Like a Rapt. Like any superior-minded
Ash'torian colonizer. Just like any human settler vain enough to
imagine they could just move in —
He missed the desert, on Manyrock, on R'Ebsyn — it
Of course, it wasn't necessarily a bad thing to want to hit
him: if the rage came near enough for Elek to reflect on it, his
awareness helped him hold it in. When he'd felt the anger
coming, he'd gone through all his usual motions: slowed his
breathing, made his limbs droop heavy and lifeless. But it
wrenched his gut to keep himself at bay in the presence of this
man so bent on exciting his fury.
No escape.
He missed the desert, on Manyrock, on R'Ebsyn — it
didn't matter where. There he'd been free. In those expanses
you could see a person coming kilometers away. You could
avoid everyone if you wanted to, there where the voice of the
wind demanded no answer. There, he could grapple with sand,
and the only blood was his own. Why hadn't he stayed in that
emptiness? Why seek people? Why work for Naquel in the
center of conflict? To have an outlet for the violence? Because
fighting was easy? Easy? To be surrounded by people steeped
in hatred? No wonder he had lost control at the end.

But not here and now. He forced himself calm.

Time passed, unmeasurable as floating through a drugged delirium.

At last, Jenchae broke the silence to say that it had been his custom to exercise by walking the perimeter of the cell for part of the day (*"Day"?* thought Elek). He invited Elek to walk with him. Elek begged off.

Jenchae began to walk in a steady gait, down to one corner and up to the next, cutting Elek a wide berth as he passed and humming low all the while. On the floor near the corner, Elek had to crane up his neck to watch him, for somehow, he couldn't quite look away. So, after a time, he stood up in his corner, where at least he could see Jenchae head to head.

That walking pounded on Elek's nerves. He recalled a boy he'd seen in the groves. The boy's brother had been counting up his harvested caterpillars, and every time he'd gotten close to the end, the boy had "innocently" barked some irrelevant question, just to make his brother lose count and start over.

It was like that. Constant, pointless interference — like all that preaching about the Samas of Manyrock and what all their hearts' deep desires must be.

Jenchae, plainly, could not tell when enough was enough.

Elek knew he should sit down, make his body go limp. But how could you lie slumped by someone's feet, right in range of any idle kick? He should turn his eyes away, but there was nowhere to turn them. The tiles themselves were little screens playing out Jenchae's circumnavigation. To distract his thoughts, he numbered the laps each time Jenchae walked by him. He counted eight. Then, on lap nine, Jenchae wobbled in too close.

That was more than anyone could take.

Elek's hand flashed to Jenchae's throat, hurling him around to pin him back against the wall.

As soon as it happened, Elek was fighting it — if he hadn't, Jenchae's neck would have snapped in a second. Elek tried to relax his grip. He succeeded only in stopping the squeezing. There his hand stayed, frozen like a collar of stone on

Jenchae. The old man gasped and struggled; his thrashing rocked Elek a little, not enough to unbalance him.

He's going to die. He's going to die while I'm standing here trying to let him go.

Jenchae was gurgling. Elek tried to imagine himself a wet rag, forceless and pliable. He ached; it ached to make your body powerless.

Suddenly, pain lanced through his head, sparking lights in his eyes. Something seized him from the inside — something not himself. His hand spasmed open, pulled apart at the bones. He stumbled back, and Jenchae slipped to the floor, where Elek half fell beside him.

Pangs lanced through his head with every beat of his heart; the edges of his vision blackened.

Breath by breath, the shocks eased to a dull throb. His body tingled as if from poor circulation.

Was he himself again? Would there be lasting damage?

The anger, at least, was spent.

And Jenchae. . .

Afterglow spots still winking before him, Elek watched as Jenchae coughed and writhed, as far away from him, it seemed, as a passerby he might spy through a dusty window.

What in the Ice of Ebalurn could take hold of him like that? It was outside all he had ever known.

It was fascinating.

It had to be Jenchae — Jenchae striking out with his mind. A mind-driver, an almost unheard-of power. As Jenchae lay gasping, Elek wondered if the old man had retaliated too late to save his own life.

You stupid, stupid man, he thought with a trace of admiration.

Jenchae, of course, could not hear him.

And Jenchae did not die. Slowly, his coughing ebbed. He knelt with his head bent over his knees and his hand to his neck, wheezing. After a time, Elek moved to the far side of the room. Jenchae might feel less threatened that way and, therefore, recover faster. Elek wanted him to recover. At least he didn't want him dead.

But once recovered, what would Jenchae do to Elek? Perhaps it would be better to have him dead. Perhaps Elek should do it now, while he had the chance.

But he couldn't. The force behind the violence had gone. He knew this feeling: the vagueness, the weariness, the weakness that followed the rage. He wished he could hide, sleep.

Five meters to a wall; that was no distance.

Perhaps he should shut himself up in the lav. That would give him some buffer from Jenchae. But if he did that, it would look like he was hiding, and he wouldn't be able to keep an eye on the man. A weak, unwise position.

Ridiculous thoughts. The lav was no protection, not from a mind-driver.

And he wouldn't let himself be forced into that tiny space, that smaller cell. He stayed in the far corner.

Jenchae's gasping seemed to echo round the room, a hoarse whisper in Elek's ear: not far and loud but close and everywhere.

Elek drooped in exhaustion. Even the shock of that pain in his head was no more than a distant tremor rumbling behind the fatigue. The noise of Jenchae's breathing, annoying though it was, was like finding a bruise on your arm after you'd staunched a bleeding thigh: it didn't matter much.

Elek had no idea how long it would take to reach the Quol'shab, if there really was such a place. If it was a distant planet, it might take days and days. And in those days, Jenchae might use him, drive him to insanity. Or he might kill Jenchae — if he moved fast enough. But then. . .

There was no way out.

Jenchae was huddled in a corner now.

"What you did to me," said Elek, "did it damage my mind?"

Jenchae's eyes darted up and down, his lips pursed as if he'd lost the power to speak. Trembling, he shook his head with a curious shrugging motion.

"Well, did it?" asked Elek.

Jenchae gave a dry, hoarse cough. "Pain going, and you can think?" he croaked. "Brain's all right."

"What you did, could you do it faster?"

Jenchae stared at him.

When Elek was fairly certain he would not get an answer, he went on: "Because next time, you may well be dead as fast as I can smack your head against the wall."

Jenchae flinched and looked away, his breathing still labored.

After a moment, it dawned on Elek that his words had sounded like a threat. "What I mean is, if you can't stop me, odds are I can't stop myself. It's hard. It wears me out." Elek hesitated. "But I can't. . . I can't stay in this cell with your corpse. I couldn't leave you in here and just hide in the lav. I couldn't stuff you in the lav; I'd need to use it. It wouldn't work." Jenchae was watching him, unreadable. "So if you think you can help me — help me to get some control — I want you to try."

But if he does nothing but hurt me? If he's angry? If he wants revenge? If he can only control me with pain?

It would still be better. Better than *that*.

And perhaps Jenchae truly could give him rest, like the tranques — or even like this weariness after the rage.

Seconds clicked by. Then came a clunk that made them both jump. Their eyes darted in the direction of the noise, but it was only their second meal being deposited in the wall box.

Jenchae glanced back to Elek and croaked, "Eat; then we talk."

CHAPTER FIVE

Ancient wisdom holds that telepathy is analogous
to visual and auditory communication, the
multiplicity of its forms without number: a smile,
a look, a mumble, a sentence, a conversation, a
million misunderstandings. All these things exist
in telepathy, by analogy. But among the strongest
of us, telepathy can do something unique: it can
take hold of another's mind. Makes one wonder
why our ancestors invented it, doesn't it?

Fundaments of Mindtaxing by Genydan del-Moiduzh (15th
century B.E.)

Jenchae couldn't look at him. Even to think of him made
Jenchae sick — yes, even to think his name. He looked at his
food instead. He had not touched it, not because his throat was
raw but because he was simply incapable of eating. *My body is
poised to flee, to act; it doesn't understand that there's nowhere to flee
and no action to be taken.* Jenchae scarcely tried to soothe his
racing heart. In truth, he didn't want to. He needed this
turmoil; he deserved it.

It was a betrayal, Jenchae thought. But it wasn't his —
Elek's — betrayal. Elek had never pretended to be anything but
a killer.

The betrayal was Jenchae's.

He had broken the primal rule: never invade another's
mind; never enslave another's mind. Some never recovered
from the trauma of such an experience. In some, it led to stroke
and death. For all, it was a desecration like no other.

*Our bodies belong to the whims of this universe; our minds we
claim as our own.*

Self-defense? That was no exception. There are some acts no healthy society can tolerate: slavery, torture, rape — not even for the higher good.

Do not think you can condone your crime, Jenchae, by repeating that you did what you must.

He had not known he could do it, hadn't guessed he had the strength. Blind survival instinct. He couldn't even feel Elek's mind; he had just thrashed out on all sides, commanding everything to obey him.

And it had.

And that was the deepest terror Jenchae had ever known, all the more terrible because some part of him had taken satisfaction in it: the legacy of Akhté.

~•~

A little stab in his side. Jenchae had looked up to Akhté's gently smiling face. "That is not a funny game."

"It is not a game, Jenchae; it's a gift. I give you a taste of the wound I took at Delurn II."

"I did not want it."

"But you did, you know," said Akhté with a kernel of truth. "Do you want a taste of my pleasures too?"

"I know you well enough," replied Jenchae, in no mood to flirt. "I have seen you take pleasure in pain. Yet you call yourself a Striver who wants to save your people from suffering." Jenchae put on a calculated sneer. "You covet suffering like any Ash'torian."

Akhté's smile broadened in the dim light of the crawl space. "No, no, Jenchae. Don't start that tune. We both know this universe is more complex than that. Pain can be either good or bad. The Rapts, they give us too much of the bad sort. And so we give a little back to set ourselves free." He stopped. Jenchae could sense Akhté's focus stretching out beyond the walls.

"He's coming," said Akhté. "Watch." And like a sweet thrumming of strings, he sent his thoughts out to Jenchae.

Jenchae hovered there, seeing through Akhté's mind with the very eyes of the Ash'torian below, the ba'nad who was on his way to report the results of his spying to his superior. He could hear the dragonfly-humming of the ba'nad's elation at being the one to sniff out those Striver agents in the lab.

As the man passed beneath them, Akhté lanced into his mind. Pain screeched through Jenchae. Fuzzily, he could feel the man fall to his knees, sputtering, clutching his head.

Then came a marvelous, clean silence. All memory of Striver agents gone or buried. Just like that, in seconds. The ba'nad gasped and babbled as others, having heard his cries, flocked in around him.

You need to stop doing that, said Jenchae with his mind so the Ash'torians below would not hear.

So you say, Akhté answered, *and yet I have just saved the lives of many of my people.*

It is not the proper way, said Jenchae. *But I wasn't speaking of the ba'nad. I meant leave my mind alone. I want no part in this.*

Akhté, of course, had known what he meant: Akhté who saw through minds like glass.

When I believe that, said Akhté, *then I'll leave you out.*

~ • ~

Akhté had seen Jenchae's fascination. The simplicity of that power! All the good it could accomplish.

But it is not the proper way.

And yet. . . Elek was a monster, far more than Jenchae.

Don't think that way. A few hours ago, he smiled at me and I liked him.

Then his hand had closed around Jenchae's throat — frigid, iron. They said that sverra had a high proportion of metal in their bones. Why hadn't he noticed that hand when he'd shaken it, cold, inhuman?

But it's not the bones that make his hand cold. He has a cooler body temperature; that's all. He's not metal, not machinery. But he wasn't wholly human.

That face. . .

Jenchae had to clamp himself down to keep from shuddering: those lips contorted, eyes so huge they seemed about to explode from his head, veins that stood out blue on his white brow as if his blood vessels would burst. A demon face. A face from outside any natural order — *inaccessible.* That was a soul-stifling word.

But Jenchae had found access.

Not the proper way.

And now, he was asking Jenchae for help, the monster. And this is what Jenchae had wanted. And now, he cowered and longed to cover his face. He wished devoutly he were anywhere at all but here with this man.

And was Elek wishing the same about him? Anywhere but in this cell with him? With his corpse? Or with his impaling mind? How could Elek invite telepathic connection from him after this? He was the most courageous person Jenchae had ever met — or the most idiotic.

Staring at his orange-lit, creamed rice, Jenchae could see an evil face in its shadows. Elek's? His own? He stirred it smooth.

But I can't refuse him. He comes to me for help; I can't refuse it. I must still know how to use my mind for good.

Jenchae made himself look up from his bowl. Elek's eyes, thank God, were not on him. He was gazing at his own bowl, fingering his spoon. Those eyes turned away, Elek was just a man.

He's about to die.

And he's just a child. Two and half centuries is much and yet it's nothing. Inside, we're all children, hurting and not knowing how to make the hurting stop.

It came to Jenchae that last night, before he had dreamed of Akhté, he had dreamed of his mother, of running into her workroom to escape some unseen monster and being safe there in the circle of her thwapping loom.

Will I see her again? Is there seeing after death?

Maybe a quick death was better? Cut the ties. Or no need ever to cut ties again. *For me, perhaps this Turn is over and I will have earned my rest. But, no, not after this. Unless perhaps I can atone.*

In the back of his mind, it irked him that he'd framed that idea in Ash'torian terms: the great Turns that are as days to Tra'hae. No use dwelling on that.

He wet his lips. "You can't really mean that you would let me touch your mind?"

"Let?" Elek grinned. "It doesn't seem I can stop you."

"Don't mock me. And don't mock yourself, not about this. I wronged you. I'm sorrier than you know. I will not do it again."

"You may have to."

"I will not!" The words came through his strained throat as a hiss. "Not even to save myself." *Once more, and I would lose myself.*

Elek shrugged. "It was self-defense."

Could it be that he truly did not understand?

"It was a crime," said Jenchae.

"Yes. So? We are criminals, remember?"

Jenchae peered at him. "Don't you care?"

"Care?" Elek stared back with a hint of confusion. "You knocked my mind all tail-to-nails. Of course, I care." He paused. "But you said you could help me. And now you're saying — what? — you won't take control of my mind again — or you won't touch my mind at all?"

"I don't see how I can do either," said Jenchae, not sure how much he meant it.

Elek hesitated. "Don't you care that I'm going to kill you?"

"You've decided to, then?"

"I mean if you don't help me. *You're* the one who's deciding."

Jenchae shook his head. "I can't."

"Well, obviously you can." Elek was tapping his thumb fast on his knee. "You'd really rather die? Are you crazy?"

Crazy? Yes, it was crazy to antagonize the man, when neither of them wanted Jenchae dead, when Jenchae had an obligation to help. But what if he could not help? What if he looked inside Elek's mind, and instead of showing him how to make peace with the pains there, he only flamed the embers of his own hate?

Jenchae had already proven that he still held violence within him. And add to that Elek's rage too?

But that was cowardice. If he could aid Elek at all, he could not let self-doubt stay his hand.

Jenchae sighed. *"Destusolee"*: the ancient Sama word came out as a whisper. But it came out: not an Ash'torian word; a good Outlier word. Its sound made Jenchae stronger.

"We'll overcome?" Elek repeated in Ash'torian. "What? Me?"

Jenchae tried to clear his throat, failed, continued hoarsely, "What we can."

Elek peered.

After a moment, Jenchae went on, "No, not you. Your rage perhaps." *My fear perhaps.*

"I am my rage."

Anger ignited in Jenchae. *And now — now — he's going to protest it's all futile? After asking my help? After almost killing me? After driving me to —*

"Do you still want to try?"

The way Elek's lips twitched made Jenchae's skin crawl. "I don't have much to lose, do I?"

"Is this truly what you want?"

"When?"

"The sooner the better." *While my resolution stands.*

"Then let's get on with it."

~ • ~

At Elek's acquiescence, calm descended on Jenchae. He didn't analyze it; the more he could forget himself in the requirements of the moment, the more adept he'd be at fulfilling his task. Action without reflection was purest.

He would see into Elek and help Elek meet what they found.

Two dull clunks as they set aside their bowls; the swish of fabric on tile as they moved to sit face to face. Jenchae held out his hands. When Elek took them in his own hard hands, fear pierced Jenchae. Gone at once. There was nothing but the moment. He looked into Elek's dark eyes flecked with lamplight. Anger flickered in Jenchae at that implacable stare: no guilt, not even an attempt at apology. Jenchae, at least, had apologized. Not Elek. This man didn't deserve his help.

It doesn't matter if he deserves it. Pay pain with pain, and there'll be nothing left but pain. It is right to help him.

Help him. . .?

For a few seconds, the thought of imposing his mind on Elek's again made Jenchae feel ill. But this was what Elek wanted. Help, not imposition.

Jenchae drew a long breath and reached out toward Elek's mind, gently. Respectfully. Again his mind touched nothing. But Elek's eyes widened.

Have I reached you? Jenchae asked with his thoughts.

"Yes," Elek whispered.

Tell me with your mind.

A black silence followed, stirred only by Elek's rapid breathing. Then, deep inside Jenchae, a sound wavered into being, toneless as a recording rippling through an expanse of water.

Yes, I hear you.

Give me a sense of you, Jenchae replied. *I have to feel your presence if I'm to help you.*

Elek shook his head. "I can't."

You will have to trust me, even though I've given you small reason to. If we are going to do this, there's no other way.

Elek spat back, "It's not a question of trust, don't you see? I just can't."

Then I'll have to search for myself.

"Then search."

Jenchae pressed harder against the emptiness. It was uncomfortable, contradictory: to break down another's mental barriers was an act of violence — an act of violence in the name of quenching violence. Was this so different from the way he had seized Elek's mind before?

Jenchae pushed aside his own thoughts, concentrated on testing the nothingness.

And haltingly the nothingness gave way to a dense cold, an atmosphere rather than a presence. Elek's arms began to shake, rattling Jenchae. Then, Elek swayed where he sat, eyes closing. As if in answer, a wave of vertigo swept over Jenchae; he could feel himself reel too. Yes, it was an atmosphere, a choking mist. Jenchae caught a glimpse of himself as a diver at sea, shooting toward the sun lest he die in the frigid dark.

But that was not the way out.

He dove deeper.

~ • ~

It was there. All Jenchae had been seeking. Thoughts strangled half-born, images hammering Jenchae like hail.

Outlier faces twisted with loathing. . .

Naquel — Jenchae recognized him clearly — tall and brown, as he locked in the force field around Elek. Naquel speaking soft, disappointed words — and walking away. . .

Some time before that, the bodies slumped at Elek's command. Outlier bones cracked, Ash'torian bones. . .

But no feeling for it, no emotion at all.

Dizzily, the years swept back toward the beginning.

Ned'yem's blood in the dust. No feeling.

Ned'yem in the mountains, her hair flaming in the red sun of autumn. Her arms stretched over the desert, invoking the spirits of the dead. . .

A flare of fury there, pinched out like Ned'yem as Elek's mind recoiled back to —

The groves of the south-lands: uneven rows of marula trees. Gnarled bark under gentle fingers. And yet, there, too, the rage followed, sullying —

Jenchae, you said you'd help me —

And before, the dust-clouded streets, bleached to a dirty white by the sun. The silver of sverra bones, the white of human bones. Blood blackened the streets of Manyrock, permeated the desert air. Aircraft and guns, voices punctured the ears. Laughter and the smell of burnt skin. . .

That was nothing.

But the woman with a sun-bronzed face and chestnut hair, Elek's human mother, that was —

Jenchae, you didn't tell me —

— like her, Colmuan, in the moonlight, just before —

You are stealing me, Jenchae!

It fell like a tidal wave smashing Jenchae. His consciousness slipped.

But Elek was firm now, buoyed on the rage.

Elek's hands squeezed down on Jenchae's. Jenchae heard his metacarpals snap — but he could not register the pain. In some part of their minds, they understood that this time Jenchae would die.

I don't care what comes next, Elek droned inside his head, *as long as I can make you pay.* Jenchae had almost forgotten the taste of such hate. Hatred for these memories.

Sure and strong, that hate restored Jenchae.

He would not die here.

Cool as marble, Jenchae hurled his mind over Elek's, as one would throw a soaking blanket on a sudden blaze: quenching, smothering, killing. He imagined himself pressing all his body on the dripping cloth, holding it down over some desperate, pitching creature. By degrees, Jenchae's emotions stilled; his breathing was quiet, his heart rate slow. At last, the writhing underneath him subsided.

Jenchae opened his eyes without realizing he'd shut them, saw Elek sitting, head bowed, across from him. Even as he took in the sight, his shattered hands exploded in agony. He gasped, and Elek's eyes snapped open.

Jenchae kept his breathing even — by sheer force of will, aware all the while that it was not only himself but Elek whose spirit he was stilling. He saw no more pictures from Elek's mind, but the bond was there between them, almost a physical vibration. And he could feel Elek's presence now: a real presence, a mass of impressions shifting moment by moment.

But how unimportant it suddenly seemed next to the shocks that were shooting down his fingers, up his arms.

Don't think of that. Think of him.

An open mind. Yet this mind was tranquilized by his own. Tranquilized — that was the only way to put it. To enclose Elek's feelings in his own mind's grasp was not what Jenchae had intended. Another mistake. Not as egregious as taking control of the man's body, not as thorough a violation. But still a conquest, an enslavement, a spilling over of Elek's rage into Jenchae's own actions.

That's right, blame Elek, he chastised himself.

In any case, it had happened. It would be dealt with.

At least I'm in touch with him now.

Elek let go of his hands. They hurt like flesh in flame. Like a mind. . .

He glanced at Elek.

"Yes, I suppose my mind really must feel like that," Elek
answered the thought. A clear verbal answer to a subvocalized
thought!

"We're in close," Jenchae whispered through his swollen
throat.

"Too close." Elek's voice was flat.

"But it doesn't burn me: your mind. Only for a second.
Only, God, my hands burn."

"I know."

When Jenchae turned from Elek and made himself look
at his hands, he nearly cried: the bones jutted at impossible
angles. And no help to call, no first aid supplies. He stared for
some seconds, and then he did cry, whimpering and welcoming
the tears that blurred his eyes.

"I could try to tear some bandages from these coveralls,"
said Elek.

Jenchae nodded.

Elek did try, first along the pant leg, finally taking off the
whole suit and trying it at various points. Jenchae watched,
hoping Elek's motion would distract him from the pain. It
didn't. The material stretched out of shape but refused to break.
A metaphor for life, thought Jenchae without conviction.

Elek glanced at him. "Oh, make no mistake; life does
break." He put his coverall back on. It bunched in funny points.
Elek's mind stayed calm: flickers of discomfort, relief — nothing
intense. Jenchae had him quelled too much for that.

"I don't know why I let you do that," said Elek, sitting by
Jenchae once more. A flash of something stronger: anger, grief.
You only made me remember things I'd rather forget.

We need to remember. Jenchae had not intended to think
that to him and added quickly, "At least, you didn't kill me."

"No, but if I do, you'll certainly know why."

That was a joke of sorts, Jenchae realized. He forced
himself to smile, wondering how long his hands could flame like
this before his nervous system started to dull the signal.

Elek went on, "And if I don't kill you, you'll know why
too." That was not so much a joke. "This — this way of
enclosing my mind — this isn't what you intended."

Jenchae's own words spoken back to him.

"No," gulped Jenchae. "Not when you attacked me and not now. I wanted to take a look around, just look." No point in lying, was there? "I thought that once I understood you. . ." What? Whyever had he wanted to understand? There'd been some reason. If only his hands would stop searing, perhaps he could recall it. It was something about. . . "I thought if I could see your pains, I could show you how to confront them. I still do." *I hope so.*

Elek made no response for some seconds, but Jenchae could sense the buzz of his mind working fast. "Confront my pains? That's not what I wanted. This —" he pointed to his heart "— this was all I wanted, this quiet inside."

A rock dropped into Jenchae's stomach. *He never wanted my guidance?*

"Didn't want you in my thoughts," Elek answered obliquely.

Mad gods, Jenchae's hands hurt!

He exhaled a trembling breath. "Unfortunately, it seems that's where I have to be if I'm going to do you good."

And all this time he had been planning to teach Elek discipline, to open his understanding to peace, could it be that Elek had wanted nothing more than sedation?

CHAPTER SIX

The star in the night,
The well in the desert,
The Tide in the universe.
Is it enough?

Sayings of Sham'taht (c. 2000 B.E.)

There was no refuge in sleep. It didn't take them long to realize that the only type of true solitude they'd possessed in this cell was torn away. When the stinging in his hands had diminished, Jenchae dozed on the floor. But fragments of Elek kept intruding on his dreams: incoherent voices, blinding sun on metal, running — running from this cage.

Asleep Jenchae could scarcely fight the delirium. It was a titanic effort to rouse the presence of mind to force himself to wake. Curious his sense of relief at being conscious again with Elek in their cell.

It wasn't as bad when Elek dozed. The same debris was there floating between them, but Jenchae's conscious mind didn't have to listen. Like nagging strains of a song fluting through a wall, it could be ignored.

Jenchae's body was harder to ignore. Every time he shifted position, lightning jolted through his hands. He kept picturing them healing askew like knotted twigs. Foolish. He would be dead before they healed. Nonetheless, the image tightened his chest.

But at least, when he was thinking of his hands, the itching of Elek's dreams was less.

He tried to stand by using his legs to push his back up against the wall. It was harder than it should have been. When had he become so decrepit?

Still, you have to find the beauty in the bomb blast, he supposed. *At least, you're not brooding on your execution.*

Strangled, fractured, lost in someone else's mind — yes, life with Elek was diverting.

What I need now is a diversion from that diversion. Jenchae chuckled to himself, which jiggled his hands vibrate: glass shards in his skin.

Eventually, he discovered that it was easier to stand by balancing on his right foot and his left knee, though he needed to steady himself with an arm on the wall. That hurt, but then it all hurt.

Whenever he gave his hands a sharp pang, Elek would flinch in his sleep. With a touch of vindictiveness, Jenchae experimented. Yes, if he made his hands hurt enough, Elek twitched on the cot. So the fragmentary pains flowed both ways. Jenchae felt guilty to be comforted by that.

To share our pain is to know each other; that's how Akhté saw it.

He tried to keep his hands elevated. It was easier to hold them still now they were swollen. They looked like a baby's hands, broken and malformed.

"That's a lovely image. Thank you," said Elek. He still lay on the cot, black eyes on Jenchae.

"Maybe I should thank you."

Jenchae, who had been at such pains to stand, sat again. Knees first — they ached against the tile — then he swung his legs awkwardly around. His arms, bent at the elbows, were beginning to tire from holding up his hands. Heavily, he rolled onto his back and settled his hands on his chest.

Elek sat up and barely managed, "Can I help?" before Jenchae had arranged himself. "You should let me help."

"Next time."

Elek laughed abruptly. "Now, that's hope — that we'll live long enough to have a next time."

When the pain from Jenchae's movements had dulled, he felt better on his back.

He smiled. Hope: perhaps when the guards came, they would bandage up his hands before executing him. That would be funny, in a way. For a moment, they were silent, caught in a

mutual warmth of spirit. When it started to fade, Elek chuckled
again, but the effect was pale.

~ • ~

It was curious — because Elek knew that Jenchae had
tranquilized his mind — that he did not feel tranquilized. At
least, it didn't feel like a chemical tranquilizer. He'd been calm
at first; now, he was agitated, heart skipping. Yet the agitation
seemed far away, a physical reaction unlinked to inner mood,
like taking too much caffeine.

He needed to move, so he stood and began to pace a
semi-circle around Jenchae, who had inadvertently deposited
himself just a meter or so from the center of the room, thus
claiming an inordinate amount of space. It made Jenchae
nervous, Elek's walking so high above him. Elek could sense
him contemplating getting up, deciding it wasn't worth the
effort.

So Elek walked, while Jenchae thought, *He's doing exactly
what he tried to strangle me for*, not intending for Elek to hear him.

"No, I'm not," Elek replied. "I'm not humming." In fact,
he had an urge to dance. He was as light as if the gravity had
been cut in half. "This is annoying," he added without any real
annoyance.

"What is?"

"Dying. This. I feel free. I'm locked up here, and *now* I
could live free. How is that for irony?"

Jenchae smiled to be polite. "Life is ironic, isn't it? So it's
appropriate to let it end ironically, I suppose."

"That's not up to your standard."

"My standard what?"

"Your standard meditations on the path of peace and that
sort of thing."

Jenchae smiled more genuinely. "No, I suppose not."

Elek rather liked Jenchae at that moment. He didn't
think he had ever understood another person so well. "So there
were you with your course steered to peace; now you've skewed
your vectors to give me this freedom. Now you'll die thinking
life is all irony. Is that ironic?"

No answer. A current of emotion from Jenchae twisted
in Elek.

Elek stopped pacing. "Is it tragic?" He sat down and peered at Jenchae. *This is him talking. Not me.*

Jenchae was about to cry again. Elek wished he'd get ahold of himself. Finally, Jenchae answered, "It's my poor brain attempting to prepare for its demise."

"Yes, well, aren't we all." Elek cupped his chin in his hand. He liked not being angry, but he didn't like the guilt. He kept getting pangs of remorse for what he'd done to Jenchae, all mixed up with Jenchae's remorse for what he'd done to Elek. Elek didn't understand it: the abuse that Jenchae heaped on himself for using his mind to stop Elek from killing him. What was so wrong about saving your own life?

And even if it was wrong, Elek had determined long ago that to go around regretting your actions was the sort of thing that made life unbearable. Or to put it a better way, not regretting was what made it bearable.

But now it was bearable, and yet there was regret. That must be Jenchae's mind filtering Elek's. It couldn't be Elek. And, of course, it didn't help that Jenchae's hands were hurting; it increased the agitation. Yes, Elek regretted that he had to feel that pain.

He caught the tail end of a thought from Jenchae: *Have I helped him? — can I? — or have I merely made him giddy?*

"Giddy?" Elek eyed him with a trace of humor.

Jenchae didn't like that Elek had heard that. He smiled unconvincingly and decided to change the subject.

"Do you remember now?" he asked. *Have I helped you see what you've hidden?*

Now that sort of question was insulting. "I remember lots of things. Always have. Did you think that I was some sort of amnesiac?"

"Oh come now. You told me I made you remember."

Elek laughed and snapped his fingers. "I did, didn't I? I lied." But had he? He tried to think it through. "There's a difference between remembering and dwelling. You've just made me dwell on things I haven't thought about in a long time."

"Now it's all there: so many pictures."

Ned'yem: his Neyda. Of all of the things Elek had
wanted least to recall! For an instant, he thought he would cry
himself. Ridiculous. The moment passed.

Elek grinned. "You're certainly happy now."

"I am?"

"Telling me about my troubles."

Jenchae gave an involuntary laugh. "No. . . All right.
Suppose I am. You will still need to examine yourself if you
want to overcome your rage."

"I don't have the rage now."

"No," Jenchae countered. "I am the one who's not at its
mercy. You're borrowing from me."

Elek shrugged. "It will be enough to see me to my death.
Even if you die before me, I can last a few minutes, a few hours.
Probably a few days."

Jenchae sat forward, which jarred his hands. "Are you
sure? Now that I've made you. . . dwell on things?"

A tremor whispered through Elek. "So what is it I'm
avoiding?" He berated himself for asking.

"I don't know. I can't see it unless you show me."

"You're petulant today."

Jenchae took a deep breath. "My hands hurt."

"I know. And I'm sorry. I'm sorry — but I can't help but
feel. . . happy." He lifted his hands helplessly. "I feel happy."

"You're not happy."

"Oh yes, I assure you I am. Feel me." He leaned forward
and took Jenchae's head between his hands, curious to see if
Jenchae would call it "happiness." Jenchae tensed, which made
his hands twitch and flame, though his calmer mind knew that
Elek meant no harm.

Jenchae shook his head. "You're manic."

"That's a word for it." Elek released Jenchae's head and
sat back. He was humming softly, a Yorûnian tune, the tune
Jenchae had been humming when Elek had first attacked him. It
was making Jenchae dizzy and sick.

Elek stopped humming. "I'm flowing like a river to the
sea."

"That's entropy. That's toward death." Jenchae lay back
once more.

Death again. Now of all times! Elek stood and glared down at him. "Why did you have to bring that up again? I told you I find it annoying."

Jenchae flinched, a quick twitch of his face.

One of those guilt pangs shot through Elek. And because the guilt told him to sit down, he kept standing. "Before, I was almost looking forward to death."

"No, you weren't."

"Yes. I was. I wanted to. Now, I just want to feel — like I'm feeling now."

You're not feeling.

Elek sighed. "You're angry." He didn't like the note of apology in his voice.

"Maybe you're angry and you're pushing it onto me." Jenchae wanted to stand, not lie there. But he didn't want to move his hands. "Yes, I'm angry. Angry at you, at myself. My throat hurts; my hands hurt, and I didn't risk my life to help you to watch you hide behind this dance."

Elek crossed to the far corner of room and turned around, leaning back into it. "Your life was risked no matter what you did."

"That's not why I did it, and you know it."

"I guess it's not. After all, if you can make my fingers obey your mind —"

"If I could —" Jenchae shouted, "if I could, if I would do that, my own hands would not be broken now!" He brandished them at Elek. Then, more quietly, he said, "I truly don't know if I could do it again, if I could do it fast enough — as you would say — to save myself. The fact remains I did not do it again. And I will not. And that is not why I agreed to lend you the strength of my mind when *you* asked me."

Jenchae's anger rushed up like a warm wind. When it stilled unnaturally fast, Elek missed it.

He looked down. "You did it to atone." It was so true that Jenchae himself might have spoken the words.

"Yes," Jenchae said. "Please, don't let it be for nothing." Once again, he sniffed back tears, resenting how exposed he had become.

"What do you want me to do?"

Jenchae hesitated. "What do you feel ready to do?"

It was like being back in life modification training! "That's not playing fair. You're dissatisfied. Tell me how to satisfy." He paused, then sneered, "You want to hear it, my story. You can tell yourself it would help me, but you want it because you're a sad, aging voyeur." Strengthened by that thought, he came forward a step and knelt before Jenchae. "Tell me, when was the last time you lived your own life?"

"A long time maybe," said Jenchae to cut him off.

~ • ~

They sat in silence. At first, they were pouting. *Like children,* thought Jenchae. After a few minutes, it seemed absurd. Jenchae smiled, and Elek smiled, and then they laughed. Then, they subsided again into silence, each pensive in a disjointed way, and the very disjointedness of their thoughts gave them something of a respite from each other. Hearing each other thinking now was like background babble, only mildly intrusive.

Their food came.

Jenchae's heart sank — and Elek's too. Elek scooted over and picked up their bowls and cups.

For a moment, the thought of food almost made Jenchae sick. Maybe he wouldn't have to eat. Since he was going to die anyway, he had little to gain by eating. But that reasoning, he knew, was wrong. His body needed food though his mind rejected it. If he stopped eating now, it would only be from fear, and that was not the way to close his life.

"Are you going to let me feed you?" Elek asked, setting their food before them.

"That or take up oral gymnastics."

Elek smiled fractionally. "There you have it: might be the last thing you ever do."

Jenchae bit off the bite of rice Elek held up to him. "In a day or two, if we have a day or two, maybe I'll be healed enough to hold things between my wrists."

Elek didn't think so, Jenchae saw, but he did an admirable job of giving no outward sign of it.

Instead he asked, "Where do you think this ship's taking us?" He held the water cup to Jenchae's lips.

Jenchae sipped from it. "Difficult to say. If our meal and sleep times truly equal days, we've been in space two and a half days. Rippling at a standard two light years per hour, we could have reached almost any system in Sylmor by now, or we could have crossed the Tide into Selboon, but we'd still be out of range of most systems there."

"Yes, but I meant, if you know so much about the Quol'shab, what planet do you think it will be?"

"It could be any planet or area of a planet not densely populated."

"Why? What are they looking for?"

Amused and angry, Jenchae asked, "If I tell you what the Ash'torians are looking for, are you going to accuse me of being one of them again?"

"You just tell me." Elek started in on his own rice.

"Well then, Ash'torians believe that when people die, their souls penetrate the souls around them before moving on. When people from outside the Naha'jûn die, their souls are discordant with the unity of Ash'tor. Most people executed are outside the Naha'jûn. They're either Outliers and have never been part of it, or they're criminals and have sacrificed that unity. So to avoid the disturbance, they send us to places far from any gathering of Naha'jûn people."

"They aren't disturbed by all the people they shoot in the street, hm?"

Jenchae huffed. "Outliers on Outlier worlds. Not enough of a disturbance of the strongholds of the Naha'jûn — they'd say. Those of us showy enough for our deaths to be noticed at all, we're different."

"Ah, so it does come down to show." Elek's eyes wrinkled with amusement. "All right. You were some sort of big leader. What am I, a showy murderer?"

"Probably." Elek's words bothered Jenchae. It *was* a show, but it came of true care for the Naha'jûn too. It was more than he wanted to think about.

Jenchae sighed and said with great reluctance, "I think I'm going to have to ask you to assist me in the lav."

"Of course," replied Elek with a matter-of-factness quite unlike Jenchae's discomfort.

As he helped Jenchae to urinate, Elek said, "You believe in the Naha'jûn, don't you?"

"Believe in it? It exists. In a group of Ash'torians, I can feel their minds linked together in some subliminal way. I'm not sure I believe that our deaths would really disturb that link. Maybe they would."

Elek fastened up Jenchae's coverall. "If it's subliminal, how can you feel it?"

"I'm a strong telepath, that's all." Back in the main cell, Jenchae sat down again with much fumbling. Elek did not attempt to help him, for which Jenchae was thankful.

"And why do you care about the Naha'jûn," he asked Elek, who was sitting a meter and a half away.

"It's too close." Jenchae sensed he meant the Naha'jûn — and something else. The link between two of them? Something more than that.

As Elek spoke, the lights flickered.

Elek and Jenchae exchanged a glance.

A few seconds and the lights blinked again: off, then up slowly, leveling out a murky brown.

"Can you sense anything from outside?" Elek asked.

Jenchae tried to reach out past the walls and the noise of Elek's mind to the mood of the crew. The crew, of course, would be well blocked, like good Ash'torians. There was some nervousness pressing on him: other prisoners maybe? Maybe just impulses from Elek and himself.

Jenchae shook his head.

A minute or two more; then the tense silence was broken by distant creaking: a sound of strained metal.

"We've either crashed or we're under attack," said Elek, his concentration taut.

A higher-pitched creak. Louder. The floor tilted up like a boat on a wave. The wall of the cot loomed high for a moment. Jenchae leaned forward, stretching fingers that exploded in fire.

"Inertial dampening is out." He hissed the words to keep from fixing on the pain.

"Not necessarily. Dampening is usually adjusted to mimic some types of real motion —"

A deep boom sounded and the cell lurched. Jenchae and Elek were sent sprawling over the slick tiles into the corner. Jenchae must have screamed as he fell on his hands, but he didn't hear his own voice.

"Not that much motion," said Elek. From behind him, Jenchae felt Elek's arms grip his waist, pull him into a sitting position. He let himself lean back and feel Elek's chest rising and falling fast against him. The cell jolted again, not as hard this time. Elek held him steady.

A few moments passed. The dimmed lights flickered back to their usual orange.

They waited.

Elek helped Jenchae up, and Jenchae leaned into the corner while Elek paced. Both were silent, listening. Both suspected a Striver attack. A rescue? But neither spoke a word.

Then a grinding noise. Jenchae braced himself to be pitched on the ground.

But the sound was the door sliding open.

CHAPTER SEVEN

Three sides signify possibility beyond mere "yes"
or "no." Three axes mark three-dimensionality in
thought as well as space. This is why we
represent Perspective by the triangle.

Fundamental Precepts of Dwo explicated by Jûz
Lagadágaw (281 B.E.)

It happened too fast for Jenchae to react. Blinding light
from the hall. A guard pushed a silhouetted woman into the
cell. Halfway through the motion, Elek darted for the door but
bumped into the woman. In the time it took him to push past
her, the door had closed again. Elek spun round to face them
and rapped his palm on the door. His eyes met Jenchae's.

"We're not on top of things, Jenchae. That could have
been our only chance."

The woman was standing in the middle of the room,
stock still, eying them. A part-sverra, like Elek, big eyes, white
skin, shoulder-length hair brown or blonde in the muddy light.

"What's going on out there?" Elek asked her.

"You wouldn't get out that way," she answered in
accented Ash'torian. "Whatever happened to the ship, the
Ash'torians are still in charge of it."

"What did you see?"

The woman's face was quivering. "Not much. When we
were hit, my cell started to depressurize. I felt like my head was
going to explode. Finally, a guard came and rushed me through
some passages and, uh, doors to where the pressure was better."

"Did you see many personnel?" pressed Elek.

"There were lots of guards rushing around."

"Doing what?"

"I don't know! They were running around — fast, I mean, but not panicking. The guard put me in here." She was clenching her hands so tight her knuckles showed lines of red. "The lights. . . the lights are up full strength in parts of the ship. I saw that."

Elek was staring at her. His mind racing over the idea of escape, he didn't see the unnaturalness of his staring.

"Well," said Jenchae. "We'll have to wait. Perhaps we should be glad life just regained a little uncertainty."

The woman frowned at him. "What happened to your hands?"

Jenchae and Elek exchanged a glance. The woman's eyes darted between them, froze on Elek. Her body was rigid, poised to flee — or strike.

"He won't hurt you," said Jenchae.

She backed into the farthest corner from Elek and sat down.

We have to do better than this, Jenchae thought. His instinct was to go to her. But to struggle up, cross to her, and struggle back down would be grotesque. And he'd just as soon avoid the pain.

So he sought her eyes from across the room. "What's your name?"

"Meravyn. . . Meravyn Sanston."

"Meravyn, it's all right." Jenchae summoned all his conviction into his voice. "We've had some problems here, but it's better now. You're not going to be hurt."

Meravyn broke into a ragged laugh and covered her face with her hands.

A chuckle burst from Jenchae too. Yes, on her way to execution — but not going to be hurt.

" — by us," he amended.

Meravyn lifted her head, wiping away tracks of tears. She glanced over Jenchae's shoulder to Elek, who was looming now near the corner diagonally opposite her, his thoughts dark and unamused.

"How long have you been on this transport?" Elek asked her.

"Oh, five meals — that's all I can measure by."

"Same as me," said Elek to himself.

"What are your names?" asked Meravyn.

"Jenchae; this is Elek. We —"

"You embarked when this ship was grounded on Lane'bib?" Elek cut him off.

"We all did," said Jenchae.

"Just making certain."

Meravyn glanced between them. "I couldn't have said. I was transferred to some station from another transport. I never saw what was outside. The transport — the first one — came from Delurn I."

"What are you driving at, Elek?" asked Jenchae, impatient with Elek's abruptness.

"I'm exploring the possibility of escape, if you don't mind. The transport's been attacked. The attackers may try to free us. As soon as we're out of this cell, we need to know where we are, where we should be going. And I don't want to just wait to be rescued, Jenchae. For all I know, our rescuers might shoot me."

"Why would they?" asked Meravyn.

"They put me here: the Strivers I worked with."

"For what?"

"Murder."

Meravyn looked tensely to Jenchae.

Jenchae said to Elek, "It's doubtful that any random group of Strivers would know of you. I didn't."

Elek laughed. "Here I thought we'd determined that I was a 'showy murderer.'"

"Who did you kill?" asked Meravyn.

Elek sat down in his corner. "Meravyn, I cannot convey how much I don't want to go into it again."

"He won't hurt you," Jenchae added when Elek neglected to say it.

Meravyn sat rigid.

Elek pressed his hand to his mouth and said to Jenchae, "We've got to be ready if we have another chance to escape."

"I agree," said Meravyn, eyes on Jenchae. "But it will be hard for you with your hands."

Jenchae shrugged. "It is as it is. I'm done planning for my future."

He could feel Elek smile, and looking at him, he saw it was so. *Yes, you've put aside all worldly concerns, haven't you, Jenchae?*

Jenchae almost laughed. "Evidently more than you!"

Meravyn was glancing between them again with an expression of consternation. Then, her mouth turned in a trace of a smile.

"Are you a hypertelepath?" she asked Jenchae.

"No. But my father was close to it."

"I can feel you're strong. Why are you two tied so close?"

There was no point in not telling the truth. Jenchae took a breath and outlined the situation: "Elek has had trouble controlling his anger. I got in contact with his mind to help him control it. And we've managed it together. You are safe with us — as much as you would be anywhere on this ship."

Left a lot out there, Elek thought at him, but he kept silent.

Meravyn drew her knees up as if to curl herself in a ball.

"And you?" said Jenchae. "I wonder if you'd tell us what brought you here?"

Elek laughed.

Jenchae turned to him. "What?"

"You never talk to me that politely, Jenchae. That was a very polite question. Very polite, very formal: very like a real Rapt would put it. Only a real Rapt would say, 'Is it conceivable that you might be willing to share some aspect of your prior situation leading up to your present predicament?' or something."

He smiled at Meravyn. And even through the noise of his bond with Elek — and even through her own blocks — Jenchae could feel that smile chill her.

"I —" She sighed. "I blew up an Ash'torian light-ship — a small one."

"Good for you," said Elek. He was aware that he was bothering her now and chose to continue for reasons unclear to both Jenchae and himself.

"I didn't mean to. I meant to disable its — what is it in Ash'torian? — propulsion. Propulsion system. But I'm not an expert with weapons or Ash'torian ship design. It exploded; it killed five people. I didn't want to. Only I had to," she added low as if to herself. "Or else they were going to arrest my husband. That makes sense, doesn't it?"

"Yes," said Jenchae. *As much sense as anything.*

"What did they want your husband for?" asked Elek.

Meravyn eyed the floor tiles. "It's a long story. He was an HT, like your father" — she made no move to look at Jenchae. "Ash'tor thought he was useful. He was going to defect to Ranlax; they didn't want to let him."

"That wasn't a long story at all," Elek commented, for no reason other than to be irritating.

"Where is he now?" asked Jenchae.

"In Ranlax, I suppose. I bought him enough time to get away."

"And he let you pay for it, it sounds like," said Elek.

She glared at him, her jaw locked hard. "It is not that simple!" Suddenly, she shot a nervous glance at Jenchae. He didn't have to read her mind to catch the thought. You don't aim that tone at a murderer.

"It's all right, Meravyn," Jenchae said. "We don't stand on any ceremony here —"

"That we certainly don't," put in Elek.

"You can say anything you want. Besides," he glanced at Elek, "I have him in hand." Immediately, he was ashamed of the words.

Elek was sizzling under the surface with something akin to a hysterical amusement. "You can never say anything you want, Jenchae, not even when you're all alone with yourself."

Meravyn gave Elek a measuring look. To Jenchae, she said, "Shouldn't we be trying to escape? Maybe whatever happened on the ship did something to our cell we can use."

Jenchae doubted it, but they might as well try. There was little he himself could do but stagger up, peer at the ceiling, decide it was impenetrable, and stagger down to his knees again. For some time, however, Elek and Meravyn crept around the cell, examining the wall box, the cot, the lav, the crevices between the tiles, listening at the walls, the door, tapping, hammering — they discovered nothing.

Meravyn slumped next to the wall box and lowered her head in her hands. It made Jenchae feel tired, joints aching, hands burning as he maneuvered himself off his knees and scooted over to sit against the opposite wall. Their fatigue infected Elek too. His mind grew muted, the sizzling of a few minutes before almost vanished.

~•~

Her hair was the color of honey — so Elek guessed — not a color of the desert, not a color of the Trals. He wished he could see her in proper light. She was mostly human — that was plain not just from the hair but the shape of her eyes and hue of her skin, and though there were age-lines around her eyes and mouth, he'd wager he had several decades on her.

Yes, she was a child of the peacetime, born well after the Truce and probably before the Ash'torian occupation. Her name was Ash'torian, a Tral-Sama corruption of one of their goddesses', "Merva'shem."* That meant she was born before the occupation: no Tral would name their child like that afterword. Well, maybe a collaborator but doubtful. No, she was no Striver. Just an ordinary citizen. She hadn't meant to kill them, she'd said! She didn't belong in here.

Her presence had come as an intrusion, a violation of his world with Jenchae. He and Jenchae understood each other. And she — what had she done but martyr herself for some man who'd abandoned her, as if that was worth dying for, as if that's all there could be to life, just like Ned'yem when —

No, that's no good. It isn't the same at all. Not the same. Not the same.

"Meravyn, why was your husband defecting?" he asked, because he needed to know that she was not the same.

She raised her head wearily. "Who wouldn't?"

---

* Merva'shem is the Ash'torian goddess of love. The name "Meravyn" derives more directly from "Merha'vem," the given name of Clan Founder En'zah.

Translator's Note

66

"True enough, but come on."

He could feel Jenchae watching him, expecting every moment that he'd say the wrong thing. Well, let him worry.

"I told you," said Meravyn. "He was an HT. Ash'tor wanted to use him."

"Yes. How?"

"He was a healer."

Something stirred in Jenchae.

Meravyn continued, "That's rare even for an HT. But he could do it, make changes to people's immune systems, stimulate hormones, that sort of thing. He could anesthetize people in pain with his mind. When he was young, he trained in it. When he was older, he realized he couldn't shut it off." Her words came fast and earnest. "Every time he came across someone in pain, his mind would go out to them; he'd feel it all. They'd feel better; he'd be wrecked for hours or days, depending. . . ."

She exhaled sharply. "Ash'tor found all this interesting. They advertised him as a symbol of peace and cooperation on Manyrock."

Yes, that chimed in Elek's mind. He could remember hearing of someone like that.

Jenchae remembered better; he was on the verge of speaking, but Meravyn was not done yet: "They paid him a good stipend. He would have refused, of course. But with Manyrock under Ash'torian jurisdiction, they were paying us all anyway. You know, everybody lives off their network now." She nodded to Elek. "You must know."

"I haven't been back to Manyrock in a long time, but I know what you're talking about."

"Trenod Sanston." Jenchae availed himself of the pause in her speech to say it.

Meravyn snapped her eyes on him. "Yes." She looked back at Elek. "You must have heard of him."

"I remember something about it. I couldn't have told you the name."

"You really must have been away."

"It was in the news releases," said Jenchae. "The Ash'torian government hired him as a liaison to the Ranlans to work on the Ybian homeworld."

Meravyn nodded. "He wanted to work with alien life forms. His mind couldn't reach them, but his decades of experience at feeling others' minds — it gave him a sensitivity to mental processes that was useful in communicating with an alien species." She smiled at Jenchae. "He loved it there. There were only about fifty humans on the whole planet. He wrote me it was quiet under the ocean. I would have felt so oppressed under all that liquid, but for him. . . it was just 'quiet.'"

She was silent several seconds. "Then, when the news story had played off — played out, I mean — the Ash'torians wanted him back on Manyrock as their cooperative pet sverra. He petitioned to stay, but they wouldn't let him. He petitioned the Ranlans for asylum, but there was some confusion about their jurisdiction on the Ybian Homeworld."

"Did he petition the Ybians?" asked Jenchae.

"He tried, but the Ranlans opposed it. It's against their policy to involve the Ybians in human political affairs. And I don't think the Ybians quite understood what he was asking them. So he asked me to keep pressing Ash'tor on his behalf. I tried — I went all the way to the Policy Offices on R'Aej — but they wouldn't listen. They sent a ship to pick him up. Some friends helped me steal a ship from the Manyrock Defense Fleet, and I followed."

She stopped.

Elek waited a second, then prompted, "And he escaped."

"Yes."

"You saw the ship leave."

"Yes."

"Do you know it was his?"

Meravyn gave him a hard, narrow look. "My sister told me she'd heard from him. When I was in custody."

"What did she hear?"

"That he was all right. He was in Ranlax. What are you sifting for?"

"So you shot down the Rapts, and he just left you there."

"The Ash'torian ship was gone," snapped Meravyn. "I'm sure he thought I'd be safe."

"*I'm* sure the Ash'torians were tailing you from the moment you stole that ship."

"He couldn't have known that."

"Couldn't he?" Elek chuckled. "I'd say it was fairly obvious — or would be if he'd bothered to com his thanks to the ship that saved him."

Meravyn glared, her mouth a stiff, black line. Yes, Elek thought with a touch of satisfaction, he had hit the right frequency there: her husband hadn't bothered to com her ship. Otherwise, she wouldn't have needed her sister to verify that he'd escaped. A charming man, that healer.

And she'd given her life for him. Elek dropped his eyes, dampened by a sudden wave of embarrassment. Why was he hurting her like this? His question or Jenchae's?

He glanced at Jenchae, who was watching him closely.

Let her hear the truth, Elek thought at him. Shrugging off his discomfort, he pressed: "Did your sister tell him about you?"

"Of course."

"And he promised to help get you a pardon, of course."

"He's in *Ranlax*," said Meravyn. "He's a refugee there. He's a criminal here. What do you suggest he —?" Meravyn stopped and looked away.

There was fear in her tight posture. Afraid to antagonize Elek. And she should be, he reflected, if not for Jenchae. He could feel Jenchae like a hand on his chest pressing him to the floor.

"He should have tried," Elek said. "Like you did."

CHAPTER EIGHT

She had vowed not to dance, and yet she danced.
The honor of Merha'vem En'zah is that she gave
up her honor to save her family. It is a simple
story to understand, almost impossible to live. It
is why her given name means "love."

Commentaries on the Clan Founders by Denned Jenchae (2075 A.E.)

Try. Try and kill.

Meravyn sat with her back to the wall and her head on her knees, eyes closed, trying not to see.

I deserve to die. The ship had exploded like a sun, silent as lightning in the night, and the only thunder that had followed was the blood inside her head. It seemed it never stopped now, the pounding blood, reminding her she was alive.

Five people. It didn't matter that they were Ash'torians. There was a lot to hate about Ash'tor, about a lot of Ash'torians too. But at bottom, one had to know, body by body, they were just people. Three men, two women. None over the rank of ba'nad*. Soldiers doing their duty. She didn't know their names. She had heard the names at her trial, but she couldn't remember them. Damned, long Ash'torian names! One was Ah'me. She could remember that because it was a Clan-Founder name. It was a family name, a working name: one of the men, one of the women? There was no way to tell. She didn't remember who'd been what rank. Ba'nad Ah'me? Yad Ah'me?

* Military ranks in Ash'tor from lowest to highest are yad, ba'nad, sy'gad, and he'jad.

Translator's Note

She pictured a woman: a youngish woman with reddish skin and brown hair like many Ash'torians, tall and thin. And with family. Almost everyone kept close kin-ties in Ash'tor, even with people they hated. Maybe she hated her mother, loved her aunt, ignored her husband, raised a son with her lover. Her orphan. His name wouldn't be Ah'me. He'd have her given name as a matronymic, but since Meravyn couldn't remember the name, she'd never know. She might meet him and never guess.

But she wouldn't meet him. Because in a few days or a few hours or few minutes, she'd be dead.

Maybe that man, Elek, would kill her. He was abnormal; that was plain. Safely controlled by Jenchae? Perhaps. He hadn't done anything truly threatening.

But if he did? She would rather die by execution than —

The thought was a vice around her chest. And she hated herself for her terror because she deserved to die.

But I did not mean it!

But thou fired on them, she answered herself.

I only meant to disable them.

And what would that have meant to thee if one of them had blown Trenod's ship out of sky?

She'd have hated them, ten times more than she hated them now. As all those families must hate her. She dreamed of them, of trying to explain, while they spit back her murdering in her face.

And they were right.

At least Trenod had gotten away. Maybe the Ranlans could help him. They had all sorts of medical tech; maybe they could modify his brain so he wouldn't be in so much pain. Maybe it would be a good life for him at last.

And she was happy at that thought because he deserved it. He deserved better. And yet, there was a knot of fury embedded too deep that whispered that he had abandoned her here, that he didn't care, that he'd never cared. She wanted to hit that Elek for saying it because he didn't know him, and it wasn't true. And what right did he have to speak her own thoughts to her? A killer like that had no right to anything.

A killer like her. . .

No, Trenod wasn't like that. His face floated before her as clear as if she had just closed her eyes on it, even though in the past ten years, she'd only seen him face-to-face four times. It was the force of all those years before. One hundred and thirty-seven years, since she'd been a girl in college, they had been together.

And if most of those years had been a trip downhill as his suffering had grown, so be it. The love had grown too.

~ • ~

It had been a spring day in the mountains, high up above the worst of the heat, a sunrise climbing toward the flat horizon far below. Meravyn was watching the tiny, tough flowers called mouse's cups as the wakening light brightened their grays into lavender.

"Look, Mer," he said as they sat side by side. "The air yonder's quite the pink of a rose petal." An observation millions had made millions of times, yet there was such revelation in his boyish voice. He was like that when something interested him. "Fancy that light shining through dust can make the same hue as a flower." There he was, walking in the path of her flower thoughts. She felt him smile, his arm round her waist, his chin on her shoulder, his mind, as ever, in hers — and he didn't rail against it then because she was happy, and he was happy, and their minds were as one.

~ • ~

He had tried so hard to be good to her, until he'd been too exhausted to try anymore.

She was tired. She glanced up and saw Elek and Jenchae sitting near the corner down the wall from her, staring at each other, dozens of little shifts in expression passing over their faces. They were talking with their minds — arguing, if she was any judge.

Or maybe it was something different; maybe that was what it looked like when Jenchae was battling Elek's anger.

She shivered, imaging herself under his hands. It was nauseating, being locked in here with him.

They were looking away from each other now, Elek scowling at the floor.

"I don't think you know what you want from me," he said.

Meravyn tensed, wondering if the words were directed at her. She froze like a fennec in a spotlight.

But Jenchae said, "I want you to keep a sense of proportion, that's all."

"That's all, is it?"

Jenchae threw an uncertain glance at Meravyn.

"Is it about me?" Meravyn blurted.

Elek's head snapped toward her. "You think highly of yourself, don't you?"

Meravyn didn't know what to say, and rather than risk angering him, she kept quiet.

An awkward pause.

Then, Jenchae said, "He didn't mean to speak harshly of your husband, Meravyn."

"Yes. I did," said Elek. "And would you kindly not apologize for me as if I were a child."

Jenchae ignored him. "He was thinking of something else."

Elek fixed Jenchae with a glare of utter malice.

She could feel a flutter of thought burst between them.

At length, Elek glanced at Meravyn. "His problem is that he just wants to hear the story of my life. He's a welter of idle curiosity, that's all."

Jenchae smirked. "Say it's true. Maybe I'm just bored. Would you rather hear the story of my life, Elek?"

Meravyn was too anxious to be amused. "Can't you tell what you want about his life from looking into his mind, Jenchae?"

Jenchae shook his head with a sudden, sad frown. "I only see pieces — you know how it goes."

"And pieces aren't enough? You want to know everything?" "The trouble is I half suspect that's all that he sees." He chuckled, but the laugh sounded forced. "So, Elek, prove you know yourself, and let's have a story. It will give you strength of spirit, I think, to frame yourself in words."

"I never claimed to know myself."

Bizarre, this. Beyond bizarre. Truly, never had Meravyn seen two people like this. They might have been performing some incomprehensible religious parable of a theater piece from Leddra.

"I think you're both insane," she said, and was instantly glad she'd said it.

Jenchae laughed, and Meravyn smiled.

And Elek smiled too. "Not far off." He paused. "Your story about your husband, how you ended up here on account of him, it raised my hackles a bit; it wasn't your fault."

"Gracious of you." Meravyn wasn't very frightened now, though she couldn't have articulated what had changed.

Elek seemed not to have heard her. "You reminded me of someone I knew. It's silly; it wasn't the same at all."

"Who?" asked Meravyn, stifling apprehension.

"No, it doesn't matter."

They all fell silent.

After a while, Meravyn noted that she'd lapsed into that half-asleep, disjointed thinking she hated. Flickers of Trenod's oval face, his black eyes, stings of fear at the thought of death, recollections of Manyrock, of rhododendrons, Nel's tail whapping against her leg, homesickness so strong it almost doubled her over. Longing for home, for Trenod. Her recollections crystallized around the last time she'd seen him.

~ • ~

For a minute or more, he had ruffled Nel's fur, crooning as Nel sniffed him and swished his tail against the floor. Trenod had always had great affection for creatures whose minds were closed to him.

"I like thy new dog," he said and, standing, pretended to make a scrupulous inspection of the corners of her center room.

Meravyn didn't mention she'd had Nel for five years.

Yet Trenod turned to her with a quick smile. "Well, at least the place is new, right?" He nodded at the room.

"Just three months in."

Trenod went back to gazing around, his arms crossed tight against his chest in the in the same old self-protective way.

"Better insulated than the last," he said. "Thou's done well for thyself."

Meravyn leaned on the back of a chair close to him. "'Tis said there's money in water. It seems that includes botanical gardens established for naught but to please the rich."

"Thou loves it there," he answered absently.

And Meravyn did love it, she reflected with some shame. All her life she had longed to work with such exotic vegetation.

Trenod swiveled to face her. "Oh, Mer, thou should have finished that botany degree."

"Wouldn't have helped. As things are, 'twouldn't have won me any fonder job sooner."

He began pacing the room again. After a pause, he said vaguely, "Thou thinks so?"

As Meravyn watched him rub his aching temples, she thought of all the neighbors whose thoughts must be clattering at him.

"Thou, too, has the golden job now," she said to distract him.

His face brightened, and coming to her side, he took her hand. "Those beings, Mer, the Ybians. Photosynthesizers who yet swim free and swim through space itself." With his free hand, he made a gliding gesture. "For aught we know of evolution, they ought never to have reached technological intelligence. And yet they did so."

Meravyn loved the eager glow in his face. On an impulse, she put an arm around him and kissed his cheek.

He returned the embrace, then ambled away again, stopping to study Nel sprawled on his mat as was his habit in the day's heat.

A wave of sorrow pulled down the corners of Meravyn's mouth: guilt and wanting and an ugly portrait of herself as a wretched, clinging child.

Trenod was holding his head in both hands now. If he moved them a few centimeters back, he'd be covering his ears.

I am so sorry, her thoughts rattled off.

"Nay." He dropped his hands and came up to her. "'Tis not thee, Mer. Thou has ever shown me compassion. 'Tis me. I've naught but farewell to say. And must say it now."

He kissed her lightly, and with a few mundane regards to her family, he departed like a dream of happiness upon waking.

~ • ~

It was a great relief when the meal came: mashed rice cereal. Three bowls and three cups of water. At least they remembered they'd put Meravyn in here.

Jenchae could not hold anything in his broken hands. Elek had to feed him, which Meravyn could see was embarrassing for both, despite the closeness of their mental contact. Their embarrassment was almost a comfort to her: it was normal, what you'd expect from two strangers who'd only known each other a few days. But she could tell her presence made it worse, the way they glanced at her now and then. Still, she couldn't stop watching them. Strange the tenderness in Elek as he raised the spoon to Jenchae's lips. A murderer?

To quell the awkwardness more than anything, Meravyn decided to make conversation. But how? She rolled possible overtures around in her mind. Hadn't Jenchae said his father was an HT? "Did your father have to learn special skills to control his telepathy? Or was it not that bad for him?"

He scooted away from his bowl as if glad for an excuse to call the meal over. "I don't really know. I never knew my father, and I don't remember my mother mentioning any special training. That probably means he didn't have any. He wasn't as strong as an HT, and probably couldn't have afforded training if he had been."

"Did he die when you were very young?"

"Very young indeed. He died before I was conceived."

"Your mother saved his DNA?" Meravyn guessed.

Elek was watching Jenchae intently. This was new information for him, it seemed. That, too, was comforting.

"Yes, the family saved it. They were poor Yorûnians. But high-telepathy talents are valuable — as you and your husband know. My family was hoping that my father would get a career that would lift them up, or maybe that he'd just sell his genes. He didn't. Or he died before he got around to it."

"How did your father die?" she asked.

"He worked afternoon shift in atmosphere regulation and died walking home one night when he got caught in a riot over some Ash'torian aid being sent to Hahûn."

She knew he was talking of Yorûn, but all she could see was Manyrock.

~ • ~

On a summer evening, she'd been walking home from work. A hot breeze cast up whirls of dust, which settled on her clothes and stuck to her sweaty face. Meravyn had been looking forward to the shade of her house, to taking off her broad hat and toweling her face clean.

A deafening crack sounded to her left. She froze, heart pounding. People were running, voices shouting in Dab and Ash'torian. She pressed herself against the nearest wall and stared for too long at the fires licking on the other side of the square at the Water Commissary.

"So perish ye water importers!" cried someone louder than the rest.

The Ash'torian soldiers were swarming now. Some were spraying foam on the flames, some seizing scampering Manyrockers, throwing them to the ground. Medics were arriving, pulling bodies from the building. How much of this was Trenod feeling?

Do not run, she told herself. *Give them no cause to think thee one of the vandals.*

She turned and began to walk briskly toward home, glancing sideways every few steps to gauge the chaos. With a sigh of relief, she turned a corner and passed out of sight of the soldiers.

Rushing on, she almost tripped over a Sama man, whose feet were sticking out behind a reclamation cart.

She was already walking on when she heard his ragged voice behind her. "Please, Tral, will ye help me flee?"

Meravyn winced. How could she stop now? And how could she not? She turned back and knelt by the man.

He was burned and bloody, though she could not immediately tell which were marks of injuries and which soot and dirt.

"Ye'd best go to their medics."

He shook his head wildly.

"They'll do thee aid. They can't think that every Manyrocker nigh took part in the explosion."

"But they've arrested me for Striving ere this." His face contorted in pain. "What chance they'll credit my innocence now?" He gripped her hand with black, bleeding fingers. "We are both Manyrockers, Tral. And ye come of the Strong People. Ye can help me to safety."

Was Meravyn just imagining the shouts from the square getting closer? There was no time to argue. And perhaps she could help; perhaps Trenod could help.

"Lean on me." Meravyn heaved the man gasping to his feet.

For the next few minutes she had no thought but to pull him away from the square. Home had never seemed so far away. Here was Twodogs Street, stretching on and on, like some nightmare of itself. But now, at last, was the turn to Crag's Alley, now the half-dead Grandfather Tree, now her walkway, now her door. The man was like a great, limp sponge soaking against her as she stumbled inside.

As she lowered him onto a floor mat, she saw with a shock that his blood had soaked her clothing. He lay on the mat gulping for air, hurt so much worse than she had guessed.

Meravyn couldn't tell if the sudden jolt of terror came from herself or from Trenod.

She turned to the corner where she'd sensed he was standing and saw him there rigid, arms wound tight across his chest.

"What has thou done, Mer!" he cried, his eyes on the man who lay panting on the floor.

Meravyn crossed to him. "Go. Go outside. I had to help him. I'll get him out soon. Just go. 'Tis well," *though he's like to die without thee.* She had not meant to think that thought.

Yet how could they leave this Striver to die?

"'Tis so," Trenod murmured and moved past her to sit by the man. He took up one of the burned hands and laid his other hand on the man's head. Trenod closed his eyes and his breathing began to echo the gasps of the injured Striver. His Tral-white face flushed pink with strain.

Meravyn stood transfixed, then cursed herself for hovering idly and watching.

Call Fenlen at the health-house, she admonished herself. *Get this man taken thither quick.*

But the health-house was overloaded. And as the hours passed, the man's breathing grew calmer, Trenod's harsher. The man's face grew peaceful and Trenod's more strained. Meravyn did her best to staunch the bleeding, but she could do nothing for injuries inside. And Trenod could only stimulate the body's natural healing; he could not cure massive hemorrhaging. About midnight, the man died.

The rest of the night, Trenod lay on his side turned away from the body, gasping, till near dawn, he fell asleep.

Meravyn called in sick to work and was told that those malingering at home in the wake of the Commissary Attack would be subject to dismissal.

She played a token, then, to which she seldom resorted: she appealed to her status. "My husband is the healer, Trenod Sanston. Today, he and I are healing together. If that does not suit you, I would be more than happy to explain your intransigence to the news office in Songport." She clicked off the com.

No one at work ever alluded to the matter.

When Fenlen came to claim the body, Trenod woke long enough to stumble to bed. When he emerged at sundown, he slumped at the table with his head in his hands, while Meravyn laid out marula juice and bulb-cactus sandwiches, neither of which he touched.

"That poor soul," said Meravyn after a while. "I ne'er even caught his name."

"Bacèstos. Cator Bacèstos."

"He preferred death to their prisons."

"It mattered little to him in the end," said Trenod and looked up at Meravyn with dark-circled eyes. "Mer, I cannot stay here."

"The violence has got worse. We'll go elsewhere, toward the Lus perhaps, where the tag-towns are small."

He sighed. "Thou knows that's not my meaning."

Meravyn's heart shrank, for she did know. It had been years in coming.

"I am most sorry, Mer, but I must venture out without thee." He closed his eyes and rubbed his head. "Without any folk around perhaps."

"For how long?" she asked, knowing the answer.

"For good, Mer," he told her anyway.

Every day I bring thee pain, she thought. *That man was only the grain that tips the sandslide. How long now has my every thought been pain to thee?*

Trenod rose. "I am going for a walk," he said and fled her presence.

~•~

Meravyn had missed the end of whatever Jenchae had been saying. She'd been sitting with her face in her hands, not quite in tears, weak and miserable as Trenod had always seen too well. Weak, inept, and deserving to die. Shamefaced, she looked up.

Jenchae was lying on the cot, asleep maybe.

Elek, she saw with a start, had been watching her. He glanced away the instant her eyes flashed on him. How long had he been watching? What shards of the truth had he seen? He was like the old man in the fable, who could see into souls but with only one eye.

It was too much. Meravyn rose wordlessly and shut herself in the lav. It was tiny and oppressive, but at least it had no eyes.

At least, here I can be on my own, she thought and wondered what she meant by that.

CHAPTER NINE

There is no life without land.

Anonymous Ash'torian Saying

Jenchae's sleep left Elek in a windswept twilight. As Jenchae's conscious grip on him slipped, Elek teetered. Yet their thoughts were as entwined as ever. When Elek got nervous, Jenchae quivered. Meanwhile, dream fragments pricked at Elek: colors and sounds and futile attempts to flee.

After a long time, Meravyn came out of the lav. She glanced at Jenchae — not at Elek. Settling in the corner farthest from Elek, she laid her head against the tiled wall. He was glad to have her in sight again. Though just a few hours before, he'd considered her an interloper, now she was a relief from the tug of Jenchae's thoughts.

"Meravyn."

Her head jerked up.

He raised a hand in what he hoped was a placating gesture and, standing, crossed to her and sat down a couple of meters away. All the while, her eyes tracked him.

"Meravyn, will you talk to me? It will help me keep my mind distracted while he sleeps. It will help him sleep."

"Are you —" She stopped. "Are you in danger of losing control?"

"No." He hoped he sounded sincere. "Jenchae has too firm a hold on my mind. Only it's more painful when one of us is asleep. Those dream-thoughts. . ."

Meravyn turned away as if his words had stung her.

After a silence, she said, "How long since ye walked on Manyrock last?"

Elek blinked. Though he understood the words, it took him a moment to comprehend what they were: his native language, the standard Dab dialect of Manyrock.*

"Two decades." He had to struggle for the Dab words. "And then briefly. I've not dwelt there — truly dwelt — for many a decade."

"Whence came ye originally?"

"North in the Foots of Shinegray."

Meravyn perked up. "Came ye from the city?"

"I was born before it grew to one."

"Where at?"

"A Foots camp." Elek didn't like to remember that place. He turned the conversation. "Why? Know ye Shinegray?"

"I've a great-uncle there. Shinegray is not at all waterly. But lovely — granite heights climbing up and up."

"Yea, high and cool in the mountain land. 'Twas crude then, new."

"'Tis still a new city, Shinegray Nah. Thou's not so old just because thy birth predates it."

Why had she shifted address just then? Why was he suddenly a familiar, a "thou"? Elek wished he could sense her mind over the fog of Jenchae's. Her eyes were sparking.

It must be sentimentality, talking of home.

"'Twas all tents then," he said, for she seemed to like to hear of it. "Tral tents and human tents. Too few humans."

Her eyes focused on him. "Why so?"

Why so? He wished he hadn't spoken.

He shook his head. "No matter."

He didn't like the grave way she gazed at him. But he liked that she was gazing.

~ • ~

---

* The form of Dabanè spoken as the common language on Manyrock. Though the words here are rendered as if in a dialect of Ash'torian, Meravyn has, in fact, shifted into an entirely different language.

Translator's Note

Meravyn had been guilty, sentenced, locked in a cell with a murderer. She'd rolled herself up like a pill bug in the hands of a careless child, not daring to face him or this place or any of it.

Then he talked of Manyrock, and she unwound.

She understood him better now — Elek in Shinegray before it was a city. That land had boiled once with Tral-human conflict. She noted how he shook his head, as if it was not to be spoken of.

She could see him as a child on those sharp-stoned streets, a half-Tral, an exile from both of his peoples. It was impossible not to pity that child.

"And thou?" he asked. "Whence comes thou, then?"

"South across the Lus*: from Fivewell Nah."

In the South, life had always been cleaner. She'd been born luckier than Elek. It was easy to be good when one was lucky, when one had a good place to call home.

After Trenod left, she'd gone back to the Wells because she needed something to love. The way the sun threw black and bronze down the hills and feathered through the trees at dawn, that was paradise. And then, she'd turned her back on it for Trenod — and lost both loves.

Her beautiful, scarred land.

"'Tis brown," Elek offered after a moment.

"What?"

"Fivewell Nah. As I remember, 'tis brown."

"'Tis so in part — in the summer, when the die-off comes. But we've grain fields in Fivewells a good half of the year."

"Yea, I know," he put in eagerly. "I was a tiller and picker there, some five seasons. And I meant not that it was brown in the fields. In the Nah is all I meant, round about the buildings."

His enthusiasm disconcerted her.

---

* Lus: the equatorial desert region on Manyrock too hot to support mammalian life. From Keshnul: *luthom*: sand.

Author's Note

But the words sank in: he had been at Fivewells. He had lived there in her homeland. Here they sat, in this black room, two children of the same soil. She could hear the love of it in his voice.

"Thou worked there truly? When so?"

"Long since. A hundred and fifty year."

"I was just a girl then. I dwelt there then, when thou did." She smiled. "Did thou work in the wheat?"

"A bit. Mostly in the marula groves."

Sudden tears stung Meravyn's eyes for those groves and the times before the Rapts.

"Oh."

Elek frowned. "What means thou 'oh'? What has thou against the groves, then?"

Meravyn started at the edge in his voice. Against the groves? What did he − ? And then it struck her: he'd been away; he didn't know.

"Thou's not been there in years. 'Twas much different when thou worked at Fivewells. Since the Rapts came in force, they've greatly altered the land."

"They've not felled the marulas?" demanded Elek.

"On the contrary, they've planted out more. They've planted out much of the wheatland with marulas and irrigated much of the desert to plant more."

"Why so?"

Meravyn huffed. "To make Manyrock support a vaster human population."

Elek shook his head. "One can't support a population on marula trees. They make fine jam, oil, liquor, and they fatten caterpillars for roasting, but they've never been a staple, not as the wheat."

Meravyn applauded his incredulity. Whatever else he'd done, this man understood that land.

"Exports," she explained. "Being one of the few planets that grow marulas in numbers, we've a market ready. We export marulas and import staple crops. Import some water too now."

"They're planning to wet the planet down?"

"I know not. Much of the new water serves dome gardens."

"It must be a fair sight. All the green in the desert. It must lend the place a look of life."

"Lend," repeated Meravyn, the peg-board hillsides of marulas a blight in her mind. "'Tis odd how trees engineered to grow fast never grow up to look like the old ones. In the old groves, the groves thou picked in, the trees have a gnarled, aged air. One can feel the days they've known back a thousand year."

"I loved to sit in them," said Elek. "To perch on their limbs and pluck the caterpillars into my jar." He stopped, lost in thought, and Meravyn, unseen, watched him.

~ • ~

Elek could hear the breeze of morning in the leaves and the voices of the pickers far away as if in a different reality. And when the summer winds blew swift, they wailed around the slopes and boughs like reed pipes in a divine harmony. Then, when the other pickers sheltered indoors, he'd cover his face against the sand, tuck his feet around a sturdy branch, and sway on an ocean of air. His mother had said that the wind in the trees was the song of Reason, and Manyrock had been called the World of Song. For a time, he had believed in the Reason of the trees.

"Slow work," Meravyn remarked.

"There was no rush."

"And nowadays there would be."

Something in her tone jarred Elek. The leaves vanished before the hard immediacy of her. Whispering trees became the ventilator whistling. Meravyn's face reminded him of the flat, unbending surface of their cell door.

She is a true Striver spirit, immovable.

For a minute or more, they sat in silence, Meravyn frowning at a tile at her knees.

At length, she said, "I despised the waterly domes, yet they molded me and my loves — and my life. Let me chisel thee a story." (Elek refrained from saying, "I thought that thou was.") "I used to work to expand wheat yields. Truthfully, I found it silly: this fascination with expansion, as if 'twere some law that Manyrock be as populous as possible. But when our wheat crop began to shift off-world, they had no more need of my work. Five months, I went wageless. Trenod had to go back to the health-house where he'd once healed, just to keep food in our mouths. He had a perpetual headache for full *two months*."

She paused and looked away timidly. Elek realized that he'd been glaring since the mention of her husband, and he could not bring himself to stop.

"'Tis no matter," said Meravyn. "In time, I pulled a job in the Department of Urban Water Management. Their office was all glass: blue-green and silver. And they had huge planters filled with rhododendrons. Rhododendrons, Elek! Does thou know them?"

"They're flowering bushes, oft red or pink."

"They are water suckers. 'Twas an extravagant waste. Yet they were fair to see: dense inflorescences of flowers with beautiful fused corollas, some white, some magenta. Petals softer than fingers to the touch, and when they withered, they slipped off the receptacle like little brown gloves and left long green pistils like butterfly tongues. Day by day, I watched them in the planter by my desk. They were parasites on our planet. And I loved them."

"That's how 'twas in the marulas." Elek found a kindred understanding in her face. Her eyes, big with orange moons, should have been filled with the three white moons of Manyrock.

He said, "I would I could have seen thee on the plains off Fivewell Nah."

It was the wrong thing to say. She shrank away and glanced at Jenchae on the cot.

Elek realized that Jenchae was awake — had been for some time. Yes, at some point in Meravyn's tale, the quality of his thoughts had solidified, sharpened with waking. It puzzled Elek that he hadn't consciously registered the change. And it vexed him to have Jenchae intrude. He didn't want Jenchae here, not now, not with her. But he needed him — to be a hand on his shoulder, holding him down. So could he fume at the hand yet be glad of its pressure?

~•~

Jenchae made a slight movement. In his stirring, Meravyn could almost hear a whisper, "Be careful." Her thought or his? She could open her mind to him to find out, but that would mean letting Elek in, because Elek's thoughts were tangled up with Jenchae's.

And she did not want to share her mind with Elek. He was too close already, sketching pictures of seeing her in Fivewells.

"We were just discussing memories of Manyrock," Meravyn told Jenchae in Ash'torian.

"So I gathered. Your dialect and my people's aren't all that different. I couldn't help but listen, but didn't mean to intrude."

"That's a noble sentiment, Jenchae," said Elek, "considering my thoughts are yours anyway."

"Elek —" Jenchae grimaced as he struggled up on his elbows. Meravyn moved to help him, supporting him as he maneuvered off the cot to sit on the floor. Only after Jenchae was settled did it strike her that Elek, too, had stretched out his arms to help, for all his bitter words. "You really think your thoughts are mine, Elek?"

"Think it? I live it. Every moment, Jenchae."

Jenchae shook his head turned to Meravyn. "Meravyn, you spoke of a plant you knew on Manyrock."

"My rhododendrons," said Meravyn, hoping that talk of her flowers would deflect the tension between the two men.

"Imports?"

"Yes. I was angry at myself for liking them because they were invaders brought by invaders. Do you know what I mean, Jenchae?"

"I do."

"Elek said he felt that way for the marulas —"

Jenchae shot a sharp look at Elek, and Elek froze, staring back. What had Jenchae sensed? Had her words set something off in Elek? Must she censor all she said as if he were a child? She would not do it. She would treat him like an adult and speak her mind.

She would give him that respect and see if he earned it. "But I don't think it's quite the same thing with the marulas.

They are our trees. It isn't like loving the enemy." *It's true,* she reflected with a new sense of assurance. "Loving the enemy: that is what will destroy us. That's how they will do it and how they consciously intend to do it. They come at us with their beauty, and we can fight their cruelty all our lives, but we cannot fight that."

Elek sat still and seemed to listen. *There's one positive mark for Elek,* thought Meravyn.

Jenchae nodded. "I've heard that before. But I say they can't destroy us; only the annihilation of every one of us can do that. They could not sand out the contours of us: no, not if we did all in our own power to aid them. We, too, are old trees with rings long set."

"Did you work on that metaphor a long time?" snapped Elek.

Jenchae spared him a glance. "I used it in a pamphlet once."

"I hope you're right, Jenchae," Meravyn said. "If it is true that we'll endure as long as one of us does, then we're safe for while yet — because Trenod escaped. Perhaps, in some sense, he takes us all out of their grasp."

Jenchae nodded, but his eyes were back on Elek.

Meravyn watched her words slide into nothing. *No. Trenod escaped, and I didn't; it's that simple.*

Elek was massaging his head, a gesture Meravyn had seen a thousand times. Her sympathy was immediate, born of all those years with Trenod's pain.

"I need to get some sleep," said Elek.

"Good luck," said Jenchae.

To Meravyn's surprise, Elek laughed and she smiled with him.

CHAPTER TEN

When the heart calls you home, there is no
elsewhere.

"The Moving of Mon," a song by Decodo Neäja*
(26 B.E)

To think of her now would be to give her Jenchae. But
Meravyn had dredged her up, and now she kept pounding at
Elek's thoughts until he didn't have the strength to force her
back again. So he lay back on the cot and let her in.

~ • ~

The way she snatched the mic out of her ear was what
first caught his attention. He was sitting at a terminal, checking
the maps. Ned'yem, a couple of stations down, was typing
translations of Ash'torian code-chatter. Then, just like that: *slam*
went the stop switch and *thunk* the mic on the keypad.

He'd scarcely thought of her till then. She was just
Ned'yem, the simultaneous translator, that Ash'torian defector,
the life-sharer of that ambassador who'd been killed on
Manyrock. It seemed strange that a woman with a life-sharer
murdered by Strivers would work as a Striver. But she had so
many friends who vouched for her here that he'd accepted her as

---

* Mon is the Sama goddess of love. Decodo Neäja was a Sama
musician during the Kiri-Sama War. Born on Tsoürn (later
Manyrock), he is better remembered there than in most
surviving Sama enclaves.

Author's Note

a colleague on their word. She must have small love for
Manyrock though. And since Elek himself came from
Manyrock, he'd reasoned it would be best to avoid her — no
reason to stir up bad feeling. That was as much reflection as
he'd given her.

When she snapped off the recording, he assumed at first
that she'd found something big. Plans for a major assault? But if
that were the case, she'd recheck it, and she didn't. She just
leaned on her elbows, fingers digging through copper hair, and
sniffed wetly.

Life, Elek had realized long before, was an act into which
honesty occasionally intruded. And though, like everyone, he
strove to perfect his act, it was honesty that moved him. In that
moment, she moved him.

~•~

Jenchae was quiet in Elek's mind, like any inveterate
eavesdropper. Elek snatched a glance his way; there he was, on
his back on the tiles examining his broken hands as if planning
to sketch them.

Where was Meravyn? He couldn't see her, which meant
she was either hiding in the lav again or in the corner by the cot
just beyond his head. Yes, he could hear her in the corner,
breathing. An unmoving mass pulling him into its gravity.
Ned'yem had got into his life like that, always there, always at
the center of things. Both dwelt with him: Meravyn physically,
in this cell; Ned'yem in memory with all the falsity of perfection,
like that sentimental glow with which he still endowed his time
on Besqûn.

In those days, his universe had formed a tidy grid. There
were oppressors and oppressed, and their combat was eternal.
By definition, the oppressed were Elek's people, and their cause
—which was their freedom — was self-evidently just. And
within each of these groups, there were different types of people:
some made tech and some grew food, and some found their
strength in the eye of battle.

It had been plain to Elek, then, that his mistake had been
to try to live as the food-growing kind when he was naturally a
warrior. His days in the marula groves had ended with killing.
In a calmer moment, of course, he would have had no wish to

kill that man, a man who had been his friend. Yet in the instant itself, he had plunged as inexorably as a waterfall toward the center of a world. The lesson was clear. In the peace of the groves, the drive to kill had been misaimed. But the killing itself: that was Elek's strength, his justification for existing.

So he'd found himself on Besqûn as a hand-and-face fighter for Core, a mercenary group the Besqûnians had hired to help stave off the Ash'torians. Everything made sense there with a clarity that comes when you've found your rightful place.

What a fool you were, then, he mocked himself.

~•~

It had been one of those sultry, equatorial evenings when the lowering of the sun had triggered the UV shields to switch off, freeing the ears of their insect hum, freeing the wind to lap through the terrace of the mountainside restaurant. The mineral tang of the river far below blew up heavy on the breeze.

"It was a mistake," Ned'yem said in her rigid Besqûnian Dab. "When they told me about the assassination, I was. . . distracted and took the wrong transport. I missed my ship to R'Aej and came here to Bes'qûn by mistake." Stone-faced, she took a sip of water and squinted over their table at the setting sun.

"Leastways, you got to a planet with moonlight," said Dasho, lolling in her chair to gaze at the saucer of the full moon sinking down on top of the sunset.

A server padded over, and the three of them ordered crushed fruits, lemons and mangos ripened in the open air of Fudûn, expensive — but so were good mercenaries. Ned'yem leaned toward the wall as if intending to kite off on the canyon breeze. Dreaming of flying to her own people maybe.

"Do you miss living in Ash'tor?" he asked her. He had wanted to ask if she had qualms about working here against her people. But even though most Besqûnians favored Core, no one spoke so openly in public.

She gave him a passing smile, the first she'd ever given him. "R'Ebsyn, my home, is very beautiful, and I miss it." How clearly her accent carried those sharp Ash'torian stops. "But Bes'qûn is nicer in some ways. It is not so hot, at least here —" she nodded out over the canyon " — and the gravity here is a little lighter, which is enjoyable." A safe answer. A good act.

Besqûn was one of the lightest-gravity Outlying worlds. That was partly why its mountains were so eye-breakingly tall.

"I don't suppose I could live anywhere else," said Dasho, who'd been born on Besqûn. "On any other world, I feel leaden. But I bet Elek has a notion of missing the desert. He comes of the desert too, after all."

Elek smiled nervously at that reminder of the world where the life-sharer had died.

But Ned'yem said only, "Yes, Manyrock in many places looks much like R'Ebsyn."

In the rosy halo of the vanished sun, the moon was descending behind a crag, a pie with a piece cut out. Not an elegant metaphor, but not much in life was elegant. Elek wasn't. Dasho wasn't. Ned'yem was though. Her hair caught the last red of the sunset, russet waves framing a bronze face, like a sculpture to an Ash'torian Clan-Founder.

"Well, I've got an early flight tomorrow," said Dasho, rising with a final gulp of her drink. She tipped Elek the half-smile as she left. He would have to thank her for this chance to be alone with Ned'yem. To truly talk with her was precious after months of nothing but words stolen in walkways.

But they didn't talk. For a minute or two, they watched the far-off peak bisect the moon. Then Ned'yem said, "We should go too; it is late."

Elek nodded with a sinking heart. This chance was like water ladled into his hands, and he was watching it run through his fingers.

They caught the public lifts as far as the outskirts of town. In the deepening night by the gray glow of the path stripes, they walked toward the private lifts of the Core base.

If they were to speak, it must be now. There in the open, where speech could be freer, Elek asked the question: "Does it ever bother you to work against Ash'tor?"

She walked on ghostly beside him. "In Core, many call me 'traitor.'"

"They don't mean any harm by it. To be a traitor to the oppressors is no bad thing."

Did her teeth click in the darkness? "To be called 'traitor' is always a bad thing. But I will tell you how I see it." She proceeded like someone teaching a child a physics theorem: "The Ash'torians, you know, began as mercenaries. It was important to them not whom they fought *for* but whom they fought *with*. Core has hired me because I have old friends here who went to college with me on R'Ebsyn. I am happy to work with them. Perhaps if we really hurt Ash'tor, then I would not. But we only keep Ash'tor away from Bes'qûn. Ash'tor does not need Bes'qûn. It is what the Bes'qûnians want. I believe they should have what they want on their own planet."

Elek wasn't sure he understood her explanation, but he moved on: "Is that how you felt about Manyrock?"

Ned'yem shook her head, not a denial, simply a refusal to discuss it. Manyrock was a tactless question, like every honest question. She turned from him as if he were the sun in her face. An honest answer.

After a moment, Elek thought to say, "We can speak Ash'torian if you want." It seemed suddenly absurd to use Besqûnian Dab when it was foreign to them both.

"Is it possible you've had occasion to study our language?" asked Ned'yem in Ash'torian.

"I have had many years of life to learn it." Elek put the words together with deliberation.

"Of course, you're a Tral," she said. He smiled to hear her use the Manyrock word. "You're probably one of the oldest people in this Core-cell."

"One hundred and ten."

"Might I be right to guess that you've been away from Manyrock a long time?"

"About a decade." Elek had stayed on Besqûn eight years in part because it resembled Manyrock. Now, peering at black peaks against an indigo sky, he could almost see the heights of Shinegray. Like Manyrock, at first glance, Besqûn was all plains and mountains. But here it was dead land: microbes, lichens, a few plants and arthropods were all that could manage outside the UV shields that the Besqûnians had set up to compensate for an atmo-gen that couldn't get the ozone level quite right.

On Manyrock, though, it was. . . home.

Don't mope about it. Thou's the warrior-kind, not the food-grower.

He glanced at Ned'yem. She was looking at her feet as they walked.

"I miss Manyrock," he told her.

He was surprised when she stopped and took his hand. "I do too. It's one of the good worlds." Then, too fast, she drew away. "On Manyrock. . ." She hesitated. "They killed him, my life-sharer, you know —" She broke off.

Elek nodded in what he hoped was a sympathetic manner.

"They killed him because they wanted Ash'tor gone." She shook her head. "It's not worth such losses. To spare such deaths, Ash'tor should go. So I work for Core. Here is the pass to my quarter." She nodded to the dimly glowing outline of a door. There were many such entrances to the base, almost invisible to the untrained eye. "And I must sleep, for there is always so much work tomorrow." As she moved to the door, she called over her shoulder, "Never mind, we like work," and threw him a halting smile not quite lost in the darkness.

~•~

Jenchae was asking Meravyn if she'd help him in the lav. Meravyn! As if Elek were somehow not up to the task.

Never looking at him, Jenchae shot him an angry thought: *You yourself want to get away from me. Don't pretend you have a right to resent me for making things easier on both of us.*

Well, what could Elek say to that? It was petulant, but it was true. And it proved that Jenchae was still listening to his mind. He couldn't help it, of course. Elek's thoughts were there for the hearing. But Jenchae himself had turned so quiet. That must have been quite an effort because now the quiet was gone.

Even from the lav, Elek could feel those thoughts rumbling. He would rather remember Ned'yem than that. Lose himself in her again. If he had to die, he could hardly do better than spend his last hours remembering those happy days.

~•~

But he hadn't been thinking about her when he'd staggered in from the bombing of Encampment Abte'nyq. He'd been thinking of his wrenched shoulder sending spasms down his arm and of the puffiness of the field bandages over his cuts.

All the same, it hadn't gone off badly, given that the Ash'torians had been expecting something. There was not one encampment they'd founded that had not been razed by the Besqûnian resistance. This base, therefore, had been well fortified, especially with the pro-Ash'tor Besqûnian minority placing that strike force on high-alert.

Elek, as ever, had done the up-front killing. That made sense to his colleagues in Core because he was a Tral and, thus, a strong hand-to-hand fighter. That wasn't why he did it, of course. He did it because he was the warrior-type, and it siphoned off just enough of the rage to make him safe around the Core people. This time, he'd killed two Besqûnian guards. He didn't like that; the Besqûnians were supposed to be the people he was working for. But then, if they chose to side with their own oppressors, they must accept the consequences.

One of the last of Core to make his way back to base, Elek took the lift up to the Tower and stepped out into the main exchange, their big central meeting space. Some other operators were milling around with the home personnel. He didn't even notice that Ned'yem was there until she gave a start that caught the corner of his eye.

She came toward him and offered her arm to lean on, all the while eying him with the indulgence of a prank victim. He didn't need the support of her arm, but he took it all the same, surprised that she had singled him out.

Since that first dinner, they had talked sometimes. He practiced his Ash'torian, and she showed an unlooked-for willingness to reminisce about life on Manyrock, but it was nothing that marked him out for special attention.

"I heard you'd been injured," she said in Ash'torian. "Tsoc thought you might be dead." She was leading him down the walk toward his room.

"Getting more alive by the moment." The friction of her arm on his bandages made his cuts sting.

When he palmed open his door, ice from his wrenched shoulder shot clear down to his fingertips.

"Sit," Ned'yem commanded, heading for the lav.

Elek sat on his bed, his thoughts misting with fatigue and an incipient bliss at her nearness. She returned with his first aid kit and perched beside him on the bed.

"The med level is full," she said. "But you look like you don't need emergency attention."

"Perfectly happy right here."

Ned'yem opened the kit.

He let her take his left arm, the one that had taken most of the shrapnel, and replace the field bandages with skin graft covers. The methodical way she poured antiseptic onto sterile cloth reminded him of his mother.

"This was a risky operation," she said, smoothing on the graft paste.

"That's what they pay us for."

After a few moments, Ned'yem said low, "It hit hard to hear you might be dead."

The words sent a little shock through his chest. "I didn't know you cared," he joked, speaking nearer the truth than he would have liked.

"There's a lot of blood," she said, rubbing down his arm with antiseptic.

"It's superficial." He didn't mention that not all the blood was his.

She paused again. "I'm not certain I can take this."

He reached up, interrupting her work, and drew down her hand into his. "Take what, Ned'yem?"

"This. This type of life, where anyone one starts to know traipses off to be gunned down." She was twisting one of his bandages in her free hand. Somehow, it had gotten knotted, and though she tried to shake the knot loose, it refused to unravel. She beat it futilely against the bed, intoning, "Damn it, damn it, damn it," in time to the beats, then dashed the strip of cloth to the ground.

She looked back at him. "Let go of my hand, please." He did so. She shook her head a little. "It's too much to ask, Elek. Ambassadors are not supposed to be sent into volatile situations without adequate protection. Of course, sometimes mistakes are made, but one cannot live in constant fear of them."

"Yes, I agree —"

"You see, I was not prepared for him to die. I lived with Hahbah'mah for fifteen years, and expected fifty more. We expected to have children, maybe even marry. And then he was gone, and it's like having one's arm hacked off." She rose, crossing to the far end of the room. "But life goes on; that's what they teach us. You grieve, and you learn to fill up the voids with other people. But when everyone you live with is your coworker in a mercenary cell where we are always risking our lives? You can't let yourself care for such people. Yet how can you not?"

After some reflection, Elek asked, "Do you care about me?"

She gave him in a funny, sidelong stare.

"Whether you want to care or not," he pursued, "whether you consider it prudent or not, do you?"

"You ask questions so rudely. Someone should teach you the proper Ash'torian idiom."

"Would you perhaps be gracious enough to answer me?" Elek wasn't sure if his locution was parodic or merely correct. He'd been trying to sound somehow both at once.

"I hated you at first," she answered, "for coming from Manyrock, for being part of that fanatic people who killed him. And the way you talk about my people, as if no Ash'torian can do any good work. As if Hahbah'mah was an 'oppressor' just because he happened to be an Ash'torian ambassador. You did not know him. Do not ever suggest such a thing about him in my presence again!"

"I don't think all Ash'torians are oppressors. I don't think you are. As for him, I wasn't on Manyrock when he was: I can't know what he was doing," though Elek could not help but believe that the ambassador had been a front for the same old colonial incursions.

"I —" She hesitated. "Yes, I know. It was just — it was how I thought of you at first. Later. . . well later, I made a study of not hating you because I know — I *know* — that the people who killed him were only a fanatic fringe." She started pacing. "Manyrock is not like Bes'qûn. Bes'qûn will not rest till it's

routed out Ash'tor. But most of your people on Manyrock
recognize how much an alliance with our people can help them.
Most of them are good, moderate people. You are, at heart, a
good, moderate person — maybe a bit blasé in your ethics, but
what mercenary could claim otherwise?"

"I am not blasé in my ethics. I believe in fighting
Ash'tor's attempts to occupy Besqûn." He wasn't sure he
considered "moderate" a compliment either.

She was gazing away as if she hadn't really heard. Well,
let that go; it wasn't the point.

He steeled himself to ask the real question: "Have you
been —" He stopped, revised in the "Ash'torian idiom":
"Would I be right to think you have been friendly with me
because I . . . symbolize Manyrock? You don't want to hate
Manyrock, so you make friends with it through me?"

Her eyes focused on him. "Maybe." The way she said it
made his head hurt. She sighed and came back to sit on the bed.
"It's not just that. You're pleasant to me; you don't call me
'traitor'; you don't shrink to speak my language like these
people who avoid it as if the very phonemes burn them. Yes, I
care for you — a little." She hesitated. "More than I'd like."

"A little less than I'd like."

She gave him that sideways look again. "Yes, you don't
make much of a secret of your feelings. But in my heart, you
must understand, I still live with Hahbah'mah."

What a singularly stupid-sounding name.

"I want to help you," said Elek. "That's all I've ever
wanted. I want to see you in less pain."

"I would not be good for you."

"Doesn't matter." An old quotation leapt unbidden into
his mouth: "'When the heart calls you home, there is no
elsewhere.'"

~•~

The first time they made love, her touch was hesitant at
the start. But by the end, she seemed lost in pure, physical need.
That made sense: since her life-sharer's death, she'd been living
with sexual deprivation; she'd told him that.

But never did she seem quite. . . happy — that was his impression — never quite open enough to look into his face the way that he wanted to look into hers.

And so he wasn't quite happy either, not the way he'd imagined he'd be. He wished that they could share their minds. But he didn't wish it really. When he shared his mind with people, they saw things he'd rather they didn't. It was decades now since he had lowered his blocks. And as for Ned'yem, she was of the Naha'jûn. She wouldn't think of opening her mind to anyone not "like-close-kin." And he was not nearly that yet.

For a while, they lay shoulder to shoulder in his bed and didn't speak, a single lamp casting a dim, gold glow around the plain room.

"I think that was. . . needful," she said at last.

The Ash'torian nuance was lost on Elek: *needful as in filled with need?* or *needed to be done? Inevitable?*

He frowned. "I'm not sure I understand."

"I mean one needs to move on. It's a kind of moving on." She glanced at him. "May I be honest?"

"I love you most when you're honest," he said with some trepidation.

"I knew this cannot be what it was with Hahbah'mah. But it seems a good thing." She paused. "A bit distant, you know? But closer than I have been to anyone since him."

Elek made himself smile for her. "Then, that does sound like moving on."

She gave a slight, cynical laugh. "Then, why can't I stop thinking about him? Why does he seem to be everywhere now?"

Elek offered the obvious answer: "Because this is the first time you've made love with anyone since his death, I suppose."

"I suppose," she agreed sadly. "It was horrible, Elek, when they told me he was dead. I told myself there had to be some mistake. I was at the train already, getting ready to leave for the port. And I ran — I *ran* — back to the Embassy because I had to do something, had to save him, had to see the body. I think that was it. I had to see the body to believe he was gone." She stopped. "By the time a friend got me out to the port, I had missed the flight to R'Aej. They were worried the gunners would be after me too, so my friend bundled me onto a flight to Bes'qûn. Elek, I wanted to die."

She turned wet eyes against his shoulder, and he drew her into his arms.

"Neyda" — some time ago, he'd stepped into the Manyrockish diminutive — "Neyda, you're doing right, if that's any consolation. When you've lost someone, you can do one of two things: go on or die. If you're not ready to die, you go on. And it's true that some griefs never heal, but it's also true that time and effort make them less."

"Old wisdom." She settled warm against him. It felt better now, closer than the sex had felt. He leaned into the smell of her. He'd never been so surrounded with her presence before. He must have been starting to drift to sleep when her voice surprised him: "Elek, the way you talk, you make me remember you've had griefs of your own. And yet you listen to my trials, and I don't return the favor. But I'll listen freely if you want to speak."

She could not, of course, begin to understand the absurdity of her offer. "No," he answered. "I was all talked out about my old griefs years ago." He said the last part in Besqûnian Dab because he couldn't figure out how to phrase it in Ash'torian.

Ned'yem gazed at him. "Would you say, then, that time has scarred over your griefs?"

"I suppose so."

"We see grief that way in Ash'tor. Do you know the rite?"

"No."

She shifted in his arms to get up on an elbow. "Can you see?" She held the back of her right arm out to him. He had wondered at the row of notch-like scars when she'd taken her clothes off, but that had not been the time to ask, and then the scars had slipped his mind. "Each of these signifies one of my close-as-kin who has died." There were four scars, the highest less pale than the others. "This last is Hahbah'mah. The teaching is that grief is a wound, which, as you say, never fully heals, but time makes it less until it is no longer a pain but only a

100

reminder of pain, when one looks and remembers. Is it possible you truly don't know that custom?"

"No," said Elek, caught up with thoughts of scars and grief. He ran his fingers over her arm.

Ned'yem gave him an incredulous stare. "And you are over one hundred years old, and you know so little of us. You should judge us less."

"Perhaps." He didn't want to fight with her.

Ned'yem looked down at her arm again. "It sounds like a good rite. But it lies. This scar that I took for Hahbah'mah, it's healed, you see? There's no pain anymore. But in here," she thumped her chest, "some days the pain is still as fresh as the day." She paused, and he looked away, unsure what to say, unsure what she wanted. "And I am dwelling on myself again," she said.

Elek shrugged. "If it helps you, I have nothing better to do than listen. I have nothing worth sharing with you in return, except that I love you." He had newly discovered that those words were acceptable, and he found himself saying them frequently. "My trouble is I love you, and you don't love me."

Ned'yem caressed his face. "I wish it could be different."

Perhaps she meant she would like to love him back. But he suspected she wished merely that Hahbah'mah were alive, and that she and Elek had never met. Easier on everyone that way: that was what she meant.

Elek kissed her on the cheek. "It's all right. I don't want any more than you can give," because the rule of life was that honesty must finally yield to the act.

CHAPTER ELEVEN

Those who don't learn from an error will
repeat it, says the adage. I prefer to say
they'll echo it, for what two errors are the
same?

Precepts of Argument by Bulyéra Garajegáta, 3125 B.E.

Jenchae could feel Elek lost in Ned'yem. At first, Elek
had resented Jenchae's intrusion into those memories. Then he
seemed to forget about him. But there was no way Jenchae
could blot out his awareness of Elek. He wasn't trying to listen;
he couldn't *see* the memories. Instead, he got flashes of words,
sub-vocal ideas. But mostly what came through was pounding
emotion: confusion, frustration, contentment, a jittering between
anguish and ecstasy. Jenchae had encountered her in Elek's
mind before, yet he'd had no idea she'd meant so much.

The memories hurt. Elek was always hurting him, more
than anyone had since Akhté. More than Akhté; at least their
minds hadn't been locked in together. Jenchae was tired of
being here, of sitting on hard tiles without even his hands to help
shift his weight. Damned Ash'torian cell.

*The Ash'torians give pain to sharpen us for the journey across
death's horizon. They say true servants to the God Tra'hae will
transcend terror as his wisdom, like electrons, lights their souls.*

How different from the old Sama beliefs. *For us, pain's
not a crucible refining us for God. We sufferers dwell with the gods
already, sharing their madness. Pain is nothing special; it's life's
default state.* An Outlier credo.

Different aspects of one truth? The universe as one vast
web of intersecting faiths. It ought to be an epiphany, all

102

sundering mended. Instead, the weaving was snagged and
tangled.

He wished he'd never met Elek — or Meravyn. It was
Meravyn, after all, who had buried Elek in thoughts of Ned'yem.

Not that it was Meravyn's fault. He watched her lying
on her back, staring at the ceiling lamps. He was grateful for her
kindness. She certainly hadn't meant to cause them more
trouble, and yet her presence divided them. It made their
closeness intolerable because Elek wanted her, and that ought to
be a private thing.

With an almost audible snap, Elek's mind switched
direction. "Shut up, Jenchae."

"I'll try to think more softly."

Meravyn barely glanced at them; she was getting used to
such exclamations. In fact, she must have considerable
experience of them, living with an HT — how many years?

"Jenchae?" she said, startling him a little. She was still on
her back, on the other side of the room.

He returned her gaze, waiting.

"Did your mother talk to you much about your father?"

"Quite a bit. Why do you ask?"

"She must have been stricken at his death."

"Was she?" A challenge in Elek's voice.

Elek's and Meravyn's eyes bored into him.

"I should think so," said Jenchae with an effort at
lightness. "After all, he was her brother."

Elek laughed. "I knew there was something strange
about you."

Meravyn smiled.

Jenchae addressed himself to her: "When my father died,
as I told you, the family kept his genes because he was a strong
telepath. About five years later came the big uprising. My
family wasn't militant, but they sided with the Yorûnians. They
were arrested, some killed, the others split up. My mother was
sent to a retraining facility. She worked as a wicker weaver,
with room and board as pay."

He looked at his twisted hands, lying weirdly motionless
in his lap. "She'd been there about a year when she met
Ase'qem. Ase'qem was a guard and took a liking to my mother,

Shoten. She got my mother special privileges and finally had her transferred to her personal custody. They became a couple. And then my mother convinced Ase'qem to use my father's DNA to have a child."

"She still had access to it, his DNA?" Elek asked, surprised.

"Yes, once she got out of prison. It had just been sitting in storage."

A flurry of half-vocalized thoughts from Elek: *Sitting in the storage. Rapts must have gone sloppy in tracking down her assets. Jenchae, do you have any sense of how lucky she got?*

Jenchae had never thought of his mother as lucky. The idea made him uncomfortable. Meravyn sat up and looked between them, sensing the communication no doubt.

"So Ase'qem supplied the egg," Jenchae went on, "and Shoten bore me."

Meravyn nodded. "So Ase'qem was your genetic mother, and Shoten was your birth mother and genetic aunt."

"That explains why you look so Ash'torian," said Elek: *All privileged and oblivious to your own luck.*

Jenchae glared. But there was truth in Elek's thoughts. "Yes. I am an Ash'torian's son." He turned back to Meravyn. "After her tour of duty was up, she just visited us sometimes. My mother wasn't sent back to the facility. It had been eight years since the uprising, and things were calmer. We never found any of her relatives, but we moved back to her home quarter and lived there till I was sixteen. Till she died."

"Did you stay in the same city after she died?" asked Meravyn.

"No."

She nodded. "It's hard to stay in a place where you've lost someone you loved." (There was a flicker of emotion from Elek.) "Are you glad you left?"

No. He bit back the reply. She was right. It hit him with a physical force. She was right, and in all his years, it had never occurred to him. *Thank you, Meravyn,* he thought to himself.

"Why don't you just tell her?" came Elek's voice, weary.

"Because it's complicated. Still, Meravyn, thank you; that was an insight."

She frowned at him. "Insight?"

"I never thought of leaving as a salve to grief. I hated them for taking me away."

"Where did you go when you left?" asked Meravyn.

"After they killed her, they took me to a juvenile retraining camp." Inadvertently, he glanced at Elek, who lay eyes closed but listening.

"What did they kill her for?" Meravyn's gaze was intense. Jenchae realized that up until just now, he'd avoided telling her that Shoten had been murdered.

"Distributing propaganda for Yorûnian independence."

"Sounds like. . . an extreme reaction."

"Well, it was," snapped Jenchae. He tried to view the situation from the Ash'torian point of view and couldn't. *Extreme times* was the nearest he could manage to an Ash'torian explanation. He drew a steadying breath. "I was at the retraining camp for a month. Then, when Ase'qem heard —"

The lights blinked out.

Jenchae stopped in mid-sentence, the sudden blackness ringing with silence.

For several seconds no one spoke.

"Well, this is —" Elek began, and then the lights flicked on again, firing everything with a pale, orange glare until the eyes adjusted.

"I don't like that," murmured Meravyn.

Nobody answered. The three of them glanced at each other cautiously.

It's a game, thought Elek.

A malfunction, Jenchae answered. Toying with lights was too indirect for the Ash'torians.

"Oh, you *know*, don't you, Jenchae?"

Meravyn studied them but asked no questions. After a time, she said, "Why don't you go on with your story, Jenchae?"

A good suggestion. Since they had no power over the lights, there was no use worrying about them.

"Where was I?"

"The retraining camp," said Meravyn.

"Ah yes. When Ase'qem got word that my mother was dead, she came to claim me. She installed me in her household on R'Aej. I lived in Ash'tor for the next twelve years."

"That really explains so much," said Elek, fully aware of how much each word stung.

"You mean how it explains my so Rapt-like behavior?" Jenchae made no attempt to keep the anger from his voice.

"You know what it means."

Jenchae clenched his hands involuntarily and hissed as the pain shot down to his fingernails and up to his elbows. "You despise me because I don't despise them."

"No," Elek retorted. "I despise you just for being you." He started up as he spoke and banged his head on the ceiling of the cot alcove. Swearing, he slid out onto the floor.

"*Dast* that!" Jenchae ignored the twinge of Elek's bruised brow. "Every time I open my mouth to try to explain Ash'tor's reasons for anything, you as much as accuse me of being a sympathizer."

"Oh, I know you're a sympathizer. I just don't need your obvious affinity for Ash'tor to find reasons to dislike you."

"I wish both of you would shut up," said Meravyn.

"Meravyn," said Elek, "I wish we could."

"I am not a sympathizer," protested Jenchae. "I am simply one of the few who recognize that we will never achieve peace of any kind as long as we insist on viewing our adversaries as monsters. They are not. They're people. I once viewed them as less. It does not do any good!"

"I don't despise the Ash'torians," said Elek with a baffled laugh. *I loved one. You, of all people, know that.* "Oh, I dislike the things they do, but then I dislike most things most people do — myself included. Honestly, though, I don't really care all that much about saving us from Ash'tor."

"But you fought them," said Meravyn. "You were a Striver; you said so."

"Oh, certainly I fought them — because I needed to fight." With the flick of a switch, his tone turned utterly sincere. "Don't you see, Meravyn? I fought because I needed some. . . somewhere to put the violence." He stopped. "Some place I would be safe."

"Was thou not safe in the marulas?" asked Meravyn in the Manyrock dialect; Jenchae had to scramble to follow it.

Elek replied in Ash'torian, "Not after I killed him, my co-worker there. That was no place for me."

Half of Jenchae's heart went out to Elek. And still, he could not quash the thought: *But if all that fighting had put the violence in its place, then you wouldn't be here now, would you?*

A surge of something from Elek. Anger? Not entirely. Wretchedness? Jenchae pushed down the emotion without analyzing it. There was an almost physical tremor in Elek as he vibrated under that pressure, wordlessly, as if he had no answer. Well, he could hardly have an answer; Jenchae had been right.

For several moments, no one spoke.

At length, Elek sighed, tired, and rose. He hooked his thumb toward the lav. "I'm going in there, where I intend to pretend I can't hear either one of you."

Jenchae felt like crying all of a sudden. It was wrong, everything he'd done to Elek. All it did was cause pain. It was not what he had intended, any more than with Akhté. But he didn't see a way out.

Elek huffed, perhaps over the thought of Akhté, and vanished into the lav. He closed the door behind him — but not the current of his troubled thoughts.

~ • ~

A few minutes passed. Like a mariner in a lifeboat, Jenchae was rocking up and down on the waters of Elek's resentment.

Meravyn said, "I think you're right, for what it's worth, about Ash'tor."

Jenchae could have blessed her for distracting his thoughts. "About their not being monsters?"

"Mm. My problem is I truly hate them." She spoke calmly, her chin on an upraised knee. "I killed five of them. I didn't want to. But sometimes I have to perform grand mental contortions to convince myself I didn't. Not that I'm glad they're dead — but in the heat of the moment, I was so angry. I was angry by — with decades of fury built up."

"I understand."

"But it must have helped you to live with them, helped you come to terms with them, I mean."

"Undoubtedly. But strangely, that did little to quell my hate. The loss of my mother —" He shook his head. "It was too much for me to forgive. I detested Ase'qem as I have never detested another human being." He caught his faux pas the moment he spoke it: not hating another "human" left the door open for hating a sverra, which was, of course, not what he had meant.

But if Meravyn registered his slip, she chose to ignore it. Probably she was used to listening to the human majority universalize humanity.

"Was she cruel to you?" was all she asked.

"No. At least, she tried not to be. She gave me all the privileges of a son: I was her only child. She kept a household with her husband and three cousins. It was rigid." Jenchae laughed. "I remember once, the two youngest cousins were tickling each other or some such thing. Ase'qem came out into the yard and said — " he dropped into Ase'qem's familiar, stern voice — "'I cannot imagine that appropriate behavior for future soldiers of the Naha'jûn.' And the older cousin, Ashe'bé, whispered to me, 'In this household, coming home is like going to work.'" Jenchae chortled.

Meravyn smiled with polite incomprehension.

He hastened to explain, "You know, in Ash'torian society, work relationships are supposed to be extremely formal, impersonal."

She nodded. "I've worked with Ash'torians."

"But at home they dress down and play: joke and sing, that sort of thing."

Meravyn chuckled. "Oh, Jenchae, do they *play*? I've always thought of them as stiff all the time."

"Only Ase'qem," said Jenchae, almost affectionately.

Meravyn laughed still harder.

"They weren't cruel," Jenchae continued with a certain nostalgia. "As long as I studied hard and was polite and engaged in the proper religious observances, I was approved of, even praised."

~ • ~

A memory crystallized: his terminal blinking with a message that his score report was in. His heart had raced, for everyone knew a person's future was written in their final year's performance — and his performance had always dragged thanks to his inadequate Yorûnian education. Expecting poor marks, he flushed with pleasure to see he'd exited with honors. In his excitement, he forgot his usual reserve and rushed into the family room, broadcasting his achievement.

Ase'qem sprang up, grinning with a rare spontaneity. Putting her arm around Jenchae's shoulder, she said to her husband, "I've always said this son of mine is worth my pride." She gazed at Jenchae, eyes shining. "He enriches the Naha'jûn, this one."

Her husband smiled warmly, and for an instant, it seemed to Jenchae that being among the Naha'jûn was not so bad a fate.

Then, Ase'qem said, "Our Jen'chae is a model to all Outliers of the blessings Ash'tor holds for them."

~ • ~

Jenchae sighed, the tenderness of his recollections quashed. "But Ase'qem could do no right with me. Every time she said my name, I had a vague fantasy of shooting her. She called me 'Jen'chae,' you know? With a hard stop, like that. It made me furious. I thought it was bad enough I'd been given the name of a Rapt, but at least my mother had pronounced it like an Outlier. I felt Ase'qem was robbing me of the last of my ties to — to *anything* that wasn't hers."

"I'd be furious too," said Meravyn.

Jenchae lifted up his crumpled fingers to emphasize his point. "But you see, all she was doing was saying an Ash'torian word like an Ash'torian. I wanted to tear her tongue out, Meravyn, because she spoke to me in her native accent. But it wasn't her fault she was born Ash'torian, any more than it was my fault I was born her son."

Meravyn sat forward. "You're saying your anger was triggered by an inappropriate motivation. But for it to be triggered at all, it had to be motivated by something real. Perhaps Ase'qem wasn't at fault for how she pronounced your name. But she chose to be an Ash'torian soldier, to occupy your world and kill your people. You had reason enough to despise her."

Jenchae shook his head. "No reason is reason enough to despise. That was my point, Meravyn."

Meravyn fluttered her hand to indicate it didn't matter. "We're only *talking* at cross-purposes. Our thoughts are not so far apart. You say despising doesn't help, and I agree. I say that to despise those who have destroyed our lives, nonetheless, is natural — and I think you will agree with me."

"Yes," said Jenchae with some hesitation. "But where does that leave us? Fighting our nature?"

"A certain degree of fighting our nature is inherent to life. We have too many conflicting instincts for it to be any other way."

"So we fight." Jenchae was tired.

"And we die." For a time, neither of them spoke. The end hung too near. Finally, Meravyn stirred and asked, "How did you end up leaving Ash'tor?"

The blood rushed into Jenchae's face. "It's not a story I'm proud of." *In those days, I shared the soul of Akhté,* he thought. *Is that why, all those years later, I set out to change him? To prove to myself I was redeemed?* "When I graduated near the top of my class, Ase'qem encouraged me to pursue higher education."

"Did that convince you not to?"

Jenchae managed a laugh. "You'd think so. And I probably would have left Ash'tor right then, if it wasn't for the cousin, Ashe'bé. He had a sense of humor, which made me hold him in some regard. And he never forgot that my heart was on Yorûn. He suggested that if I went into law, I could help free the Outlying Planets from within the Ash'torian circle: pursue our independence without bloodshed. My mother would have approved of that, so I did it."

"And you became a lawyer?"

"Oh, I became a radical quoter of Ash'torian statutes, precedents, and ethical imperatives opposed to the colonization. I was young. My arguments were dismissed. But I was dogged enough to bring a case against the purge that killed my mother all the way to the First Court on R'Aej*." He raised his broken hands in a gesture that looked more futile than he'd intended. "I lost, of course. I was branded something between a laughing-stock and a demented revolutionary. I was twenty-seven, and for all practical ends, my legal career was over."

Meravyn pursed her lips. "Only twenty-seven. You might have lived it over — no, what's the expression?"

"Lived it down?"

"Down. Yes. You were young enough."

"I have often told myself just that. In fact, the suspicion that it may be true has been one of the agonies — true agonies — of my life."

Meravyn watched him with unblinking eyes.

"But back then . . ." Jenchae shrugged helplessly. "That verdict shattered me. It was like pulling the reed out of the basket that makes the whole thing fall apart. *Dastusona nee**. I gave up, which is to say, I determined that war was the only answer."

"So you left Ash'tor?"

"No, not at first. Over the years, I'd acquired contacts among Striver operatives. I'd used them for information, but now I became an active member of an extremist branch. Their immediate goal was to demonstrate that if the O. P.'s were vulnerable to Ash'torian attack, then the Trae'dah, the ruling star system itself, was no less vulnerable to the Strivers."

~ • ~

He remembered watching through the spy camera with his friends, their voices softly counting down, "three, two. . ." The empty garden flickered with movement: Zahna'rem, home

---

* The highest of the nine courts of law in Ash'tor.

Translator's Note

* "I was conquered." Old Dabunè: emphatic statement of absolute defeat.

Author's Note.

from school, her violet prayer veil waving with the idle, innocent swing of her arm.

"One," Jenchae murmured along with the rest, unable to move or scream out "stop," as he should have, even though it was too late to stop it.

The front windows exploded in fire, Zahna'rem, a sudden silhouette, flung back like so much debris. To hurl fire at your own family: that, too, was something Akhté would have done.

Jenchae was ten minutes' run from the scene of the explosion. He didn't move a toe to help her.

~ • ~

Foolish, the urge to rub his hands over his face, as if he would wake himself from a dream. He'd even moved his hands up before the pain reminded him the gesture was impossible. He sighed. "We blew up Ase'qem's house. We waited till no one was inside, but one of the cousins heading home took some shrapnel. She recovered eventually." He swallowed. "I freely owned my involvement — after I fled Ash'tor with the others in that group." He stopped, shaken and unsure what to say next.

"I don't blame you," said Meravyn.

"You should. Luck positioned me where I had a chance to foster true communication between our peoples, and I threw that chance away — out of hatred and despair. I spent years rippling down that useless course. I have killed many people, Meravyn. Some I was justified in killing: some I killed to save friends, for example. Others gash my soul without prayer for healing. So I speak sometimes as an Ash'torian, not because I wish to be one but because I wish to be listened to. But I cast myself out of their circle long ago — and now they'll never hear me."

And was the rest wasted, with Akhté, with Elek, bidding them to see with peacemaking eyes while Ash'tor made war on them?

There was so little he could offer.

At the thought, a weight lightened inside him. It had been too long since he'd made such a confession — to another or to himself. He was glad he had done so before his death.

"I have failed so many people," he concluded with a certain sense of relief.

"Show me someone who hasn't," said Meravyn.

~ • ~

From the lav, Elek listened to Jenchae, listened with his ears as much as his mind, despite the fact he'd said he didn't want to. The door to the lav, which scarcely dampened sound, did nothing to stem the torrent of thoughts. He was drowning in Jenchae. But at least the walls hid the sight of Elek from the others. So he sat on the toilet with his head in his hands and let his face contort, a frank reflection of the familiar premonition that things were about to crack.

He wasn't sure if the sensation was more his or Jenchae's. Jenchae had forgotten about him for the moment. He was talking on and on instead about his youthful guilts, all the lives he'd taken.

You want to talk about lives you've taken. I'll tell you some things about taking lives.

But Jenchae wasn't listening.

Elek felt sorry for him, which was ridiculous on too many levels to count. Why should he be sorry for a man whose troubles were so trifling? *I'll tell you about living twice as long as you'll ever live with more than twice the scars to show for it.* Why be sorry for a man who kept invading his mind with self-righteous bits of criticism? for a man who was all "thank-yous" to Meravyn for showing him how "lucky" his life had been when Elek was the one who had brought up the subject of luck.

Why feel sorry at all? Elek had long ago discovered there was no space to spare on vicarious sorrows. Once in a while, perhaps, you could hand yourself a little sympathy because you had to live with yourself, and sometimes the self demanded it. But even feeling sorry for yourself was mostly useless — and for other people: that was nothing but an invitation to tip the scales past enduring.

Ned'yem had taught him that. She had been the last he'd ever volunteered to suffer for. And his heart had slept easier for resigning that burden. Yet, here it came again, for Jenchae — for Meravyn too — like a battering ram on the soul.

"I have failed so many," said Jenchae, meaning Akhté. Akhté and Elek, two faces on the same figure in Jenchae's monument to guilt. For a moment, Elek wondered if he could ever be simply Elek to Jenchae, if he'd ever been Elek to anyone.

~•~

After some time, Jenchae heard the lav door click, and Elek appeared leaning in the doorway. His face was drawn, his feelings still grinding.

"I can't do this, Jenchae. I need you out of my mind."

Jenchae glanced at Meravyn, who met his eyes, then looked at Elek.

Out of his mind. They were both thinking of Akhté. He, too, had wanted Jenchae to stay away at the end, and Jenchae had done so, and see how that had ended. Jenchae could picture Akhté now: a tall, stolid block, immobile as a fault line the instant before the quake.

"What is wrong with you?" Elek whispered, the pain in his voice a streak of red.

The veins were standing out on Elek's fine-boned head. The black eyes pulsed like a naked heart. It was the face that had strangled him. It was death; no, it was dying, which was worse. It was Akhté on that last day.

"Stop trying to turn me into someone else," said Elek. There was an impossibility in the demand that came through to Elek a moment later. He knelt down next to Jenchae. "I don't know what happened between you and that man. I don't think I want to know." He darted a look at Meravyn. "But you're doing this to me on account of him."

"For you, not him."

"Then why does it always come back to him?"

"It doesn't. If my mind makes leaps sometimes —" Jenchae made a helpless gesture. "But I know it's not the same with you." *It mustn't be the same. To love so much and accomplish nothing. . . How could I relive that moment when Akhté. . .?*

"When he what? Who was he anyway?" Elek demanded.

"My friend."

Elek sneered. "What, like I am?"

"Oh no. He understood himself better."

CHAPTER TWELVE

I am not given to idle superlatives. I mean it
quite literally when I say that there is no
higher wrong for a Mindtaxer than to take
control of another's mind without both great
need and explicit consent.

Fundaments of Mindtaxing by Genydan del-
Moiduzh (15th century B.E.)

"You're a good man, Jenchae," he'd said. "But it takes
more than that to bring good into this galaxy. More. . . or maybe
less."

Not once had Akhté looked at Jenchae as he'd spoken.
His eyes were on the body of the man at his feet.

~ • ~

Jenchae wanted to turn away. Elek and Meravyn sat too
close, each perhaps two meters from him, the three of them a
tight triangle. He wished their meal would arrive and preempt
this.

But it didn't come.

So he assumed his most pacific demeanor. "Akhté was
an Outlier from Rha-Rhyd. Do you know it?"

"It's a Leddie-Sama planet," said Elek.

"It's in the Fenlo System," Meravyn specified. "But I
don't really know anything about it."

Jenchae studied his twisted fingers. "It is, as you say, an
L-S Block planet. It's poor, populated mostly by Leddie colonists
— extremely unequal distribution of resources and all of the
problems that flock to that. It is exactly the type of planet the

115

Ash'torians love to rescue: it does, indeed, need a great deal of help."

He took a breath, loud against the silence of his listeners. "Rha-Rhyd has little social oversight, which is the main reason Akhté's father wasn't identified as a hypertelepath until he had a breakdown — more than a breakdown actually. He crumbled; he lost his head, tormented his family a long time before he was finally removed to an asylum. Akhté was eleven then and already suffering mind-pain from his own hypertelepathy. Fortunately, when his family's situation was publicly exposed, it drew attention from the Mindtaxers in Leddra. Akhté and his siblings were taken there to study Mindtaxing so they could manage their mind-pain and hone their telepathic skills."

"But the training didn't work?" guessed Meravyn.

Jenchae fished for the right response. "Not entirely."

Elek flashed a wry smile, which tried Jenchae's patience.

"You see," said Jenchae, "Akhté loved his homeworld, in spite of his childhood. He hated the Ash'torian occupation, and when he was old enough, he returned to Rha-Rhyd to fight it."

"Despite his planet's need for all that 'help'?" said Elek.

Jenchae was not about to explain the difference between wanted and unwanted help to someone who understood it perfectly well. Ignoring Elek, he went on, "He was militant. He did not object to using violence against Ash'tor. And he used it effectively; he broke foothold after foothold of Ash'torian power on Rha-Rhyd, became an icon among resistance groups in the Fenlo System. That was how I met him, while forging alliances among different Striver networks. I thought if I could convince his group to turn to non-violence, their prestige among other militant Strivers would promote peaceful protest throughout the L-S Block."

Predictably, Elek scoffed. "I bet that worked like praying for starlight."

Scarcely registering the sarcasm, Jenchae found himself reflecting on the root meaning of the old proverb: *If you want your prayers answered, pray for something that's always there anyway.*

In a curious way, Akhté had understood that. Though he longed for what wasn't, he reveled in what was: a true liver of life, was Akhté. Jenchae could still hear the singing, for an instant as clear as that night.

~ • ~

Low light. The red of heat lamps in a bare room, softened by the darkness. The cider steaming in disposable cups. Laughter and singing to hands clapping in time. Akhté's voice sounded forth from the others: a rich baritone. His mother had been a professional singer, though Jenchae hadn't known it then. But the song that night had been a workers' song:

> We could be working, working more.
> But then you would be paying us less.
> We work all day; we give you breath,
> And one day you may be breathless.
> The hiss and swell, the air so sweet:
> You'll miss it all when you feel the heat
> Of seething cells, your eyes gone black.
> A credit more to bring the air back.

Not poetic words. But the voices around him swelled in a harmony that ran deeper than the lyrics.

There's a force that pulses behind our words, mused Jenchae. He half expected Akhté to dart him one of those looks, acknowledging the thought. But if Akhté heard him, he was not listening. He was alive inside the music.

~ • ~

That verse was all Jenchae could remember. The lines spun around inside his head and sputtered into silence. His brain froze up. Tired.

"Yes?" Elek prompted.

Jenchae stared at him, until he could feel nervousness steal over Elek despite his implacable face. It gratified Jenchae so much that he smiled.

Feeling stronger, he said, "I don't know how to express my impressions of Akhté. To say I was at once tremendously impressed, tremendously concerned, and tremendously sorry for him would only be to overuse the word 'tremendously.'"

"Stop speechifying," said Elek.

"But that's precisely what you've asked me to do. I was all those things. He was a great leader, but by the time I met him, he had become so intense in his detestation of Ash'tor that he was destabilizing to himself. He'd forgotten the calm that's the mainstay of the Mindtaxer's discipline." Meravyn's mouth twitched at the words. "I tried to renew his instruction in Mindtaxing, since I'd studied it a little — as an amateur. He was even grateful for my help for a time. But it wasn't enough."

~ • ~

The river floats in stillness. You can see it gallop seaward, but its thunder, its fury, they touch you no more than the windless air's whisper.

They'd sat face to face on the floor, Jenchae's forehead pressed to Akhté's, sharing the blue-white tranquility, a clear coolness harmonized by the single warm spot where their heads touched. Then Akhté stirred and pulled his mind away, the old grinding headache sliding back into place for a second in Jenchae's thoughts before Akhté fully severed the contact. Akhté kissed him on the brow and got stiffly to his feet.

"No more today," he said, looking out of his window on the flat roofs of Rha-Rhyd, lit in a rust-brown sunset beneath the filter-glass of the dome. "No. No more at all. It isn't my path." He turned and met Jenchae with an iron gaze, weirdly cold against the sunlit halo of his wild hair.

"It used to be," Jenchae said.

"No. It was pushed on me. I learned what I needed to learn from it."

"How to stop the pain," Jenchae offered.

"How to stop the heart," Akhté said, heavy arms folded across his chest. "There is more pain than mind-pain. All feeling contains the possibility of pain. All passion, all love. The true Mindtaxer relinquishes it all: friends, family, Nation, home. Care. 'Care,' Jenchae, means 'worry' but also 'love.' A Mindtaxer doesn't care. I care. I won't dispense with it."

~ • ~

Jenchae had listened then, but only now did it come to him that there was another type of "care" that Akhté had forgotten: "to be careful" is "to use caution." To be circumspect in your dealings with people. Would it have changed anything if Jenchae had thought of that then?

~ • ~

"This strikes me as an insane place for an HT to sleep," Jenchae had said. It was the evening of the first and last day they'd shared a bed. The attraction between Jenchae and Akhté had never been primarily sexual. But that day, Akhté had spoken of pain and pleasure and sharing the two, and it had seemed they might be of comfort to each other.

Later, they lay on Akhté's bunk in the converted crawl space above the luggage exchange. Below them, through the one-way panel, Jenchae could see a steady stream of people, depositing items for storage or picking them up.

"It gives me a sense of the traffic flowing in and out of the port," Akhté explained from behind him.

Jenchae smiled. "You get that while you're sleeping, do you?"

"Oftentimes," Akhté answered with absolute seriousness.

Jenchae rolled onto his back to gaze up at Akhté lounging on his elbow. "I think you bunk here because you enjoy how it hurts you to hear all those minds chatter."

"I embrace the pain. But it isn't only pain, Jenchae. Let me show you." He wrapped an arm around Jenchae and rested his forehead against Jenchae's neck. Then, he took several deep breaths in a rhythm Jenchae recognized as a Mindtaxer's concentration exercise. Finally, he inhaled one last time slowly and, then, exhaled slower still, like a singer holding on to a long note. And as he breathed against Jenchae's neck, Jenchae could feel the people below as one steady flowing of color and sound and thrumming emotion. It reminded him of floating below the surface of a pool while a flurry of activity rippled above. When Akhté inhaled again, the flow of images faltered, only to resume again as he exhaled: the exhalation, Jenchae understood, worked as a focus for the outward flow of thought. But the thought was too bright, too discordant, too much. Jenchae pulled away, his jaw ringing with a spreading headache.

Akhté was leaning once more on his elbow.

"So you listen to them," Jenchae said, a little shaken. "And you reach out and trick them into doing things as well?"

"Sometimes, when there are things that must be done: a package to be lost, a meeting cut short."

"And you justify such intrusions by saying that these things 'must be done' for the liberation of Rha-Rhyd."

"For the liberation of Rha-Rhyd, yes. But the justification runs deeper than that. We are not, by nature, separate beings, Jenchae. A human in separation is nothing. From conception well into childhood, we physically require other humans to guide us, to feed us, to teach us to speak. All people impact one another: by word, by deed, by thought."

"But to take over another's mind. . .?"

"Is no different from this conversation we are having."

"Come, my friend, it most certainly is!"

Akhté reached down and took his hand. "The difference comes action by action and motive by motive. A verbal lie and a telepathic misdirection are equivalent acts. Neither, in itself, is noble, yet both may be necessary."

~ • ~

Jenchae was not sure how long he paused. He found himself waiting for Elek to berate him for the silence. Elek did not. Perhaps he'd been diverted by Jenchae's memories?

He could feel Elek smile inside his mind.

Yes, we both know how it feels, he thought to Elek, *to know someone else can see into your secrets.*

Jenchae fixed on Meravyn's patient face. "Akhté was an excellent spy, as you might imagine, but he also allowed himself to manipulate others' minds. Once, I even saw him seize hold of the body of an Ash'torian soldier."

~ • ~

When the assault on the control center had come, it was all Jenchae could do to keep up with Akhté and avoid getting shot. Dodge here. Dart there. Dive into a storeroom.

Hiding there, Akhté close beside him, Jenchae kept thinking that he hadn't come to Rha-Rhyd to fight. He had come to convince Akhté to put his people behind the non-violent protests. And here he was, at Akhté's heels, in the midst of a Striver uprising. Why was he here? Why hadn't he left? Had Akhté placed a suggestion in his mind?

The soldiers passed by without even searching the storeroom, no doubt diverted by a thought from Akhté. When they were gone, Akhté opened the door and rushed on.

By the time Jenchae dashed, panting, into the control room, it was plain that Akhté had the man in his grip. The two of them were standing four meters apart, staring at each other as frozenly as if their eyes were tied by two taut threads.

With uncanny slowness, the man's hand reached down to grasp the gun at his hip. His eyes broke from Akhté's then. Helpless, he fixed them on Jenchae. Jenchae could see one eye flush dark with burst blood vessels. Then, in a single fluid motion, the man raised the gun to his own head and fired.

~ • ~

Jenchae recoiled at the memory, his racing heart rushing a sudden, sweltering heat through his body. When his hands convulsed, Elek almost winced and gazed at him almost with pity. Jenchae drew several calming breaths. "That was one of the most awful things I've ever witnessed. Words can't say. Shortly after that, he was killed." He stopped. "That's all."

"So you made me —" said Elek.

"No," Jenchae cut him off. "That isn't all I have to say. Akhté was a tragedy because he had vast potential for achieving good. His family turned out impressive enough. Do you know, his younger sister became the Leddie foreign secretary, his younger brother a well-respected Mindtaxer. They're as strong HTs as he was, with the same potential disabilities. So why so much difference? Because they were too young to remember the bad times with their father? Does that mean we're all lost if we aren't set right by age three or four or five? Or was it chance? Was it bad luck? Was he, at bottom, a malicious man? — because that I know was not the case. Or are answers impossible: perhaps that is the answer most frightening." He turned to Elek. "And yes, Elek, I see him in you. . . the bad and the good."

Elek was uncertain how his own thoughts should respond. "Thank you?" he said carefully. "But I don't see the similarity. I'm not a revolutionary; I'm not a great leader; I don't live to see Ash'tor vanquished; I'm not an HT; I'm not even a very strong telepath."

"But both of you were blessed — or cursed — with a disproportionate power: his telepathic, yours — because you're a sverra — physical. And both of you have been consumed by an anger that places that power beyond your control."

"You think you failed with him because you couldn't really reach his mind, and you think you'll succeed with me by controlling my mind the way he controlled that man's."

"That's not how —" Jenchae began. Then it struck him he hadn't told Elek the soldier had been male. That frightened him: Elek had pulled the very pictures from his brain and not even seemed conscious of doing so.

Of course, Elek was conscious of it by now; their thoughts were ticking it over together.

"Look," said Elek, "you have to let me go."

"I want to let you go," said Jenchae, "but if you kill us?" If he lost his only chance to teach Elek —

"Surprise, Jenchae. You're going to die anyway."

"But to die like that? I've been under your hands, Elek. And you ask me to put myself there again?"

Elek gave a slight, snide laugh. "That's a weak case, isn't it? You could stop me. You did it before."

"You what?" demanded Meravyn. "Stopped him how?" She must guess how Jenchae had seized Elek's mind. The wife of an HT, she knew exactly how egregious an act that was.

"No," said Jenchae. "I could not, I would not, do that again."

"What?" Meravyn's voice was cold.

No one answered her; there was no need.

"You hypocrite, Jenchae," snapped Elek, "claiming you're too noble to control my mind, even for an instant, even to save us, but you're holding me in your palm right now as we speak. You told me you'd help me. You never said you'd just take me over."

"Elek, I am not!"

"What kind of help is — ?"

"If you haven't noticed," Jenchae interrupted, "you're in full control of all you say and do —"

"No, I'm not."

"I'm dampening your moods — just a little. That's all."

122

Jenchae got a sudden image of steel melting in a volcanic heat. "I can't sacrifice myself to this," said Elek.

The futility of it seemed as inescapable suddenly as the walls of their cell. "I know. But what —"

There was a clank to Jenchae's right. He started and glanced toward it, knowing the moment he did so that it was only their meal arriving. He realized he was still flexing his hands in a continuous background burning.

Elek scooted over and lifted his own hands to Jenchae's face. Jenchae flinched, but Elek's palms only pressed his cheeks coolly.

"Let me go," Elek said, "and then we'll eat."

"Let him go," echoed Meravyn with quiet force.

"And if he tries to kill us, Meravyn?"

He looked over Elek's shoulder to her face. She shook her head. "As he said, we'll die anyway. It's oddly freeing."

Elek sighed and sat back, glanced at Meravyn. "If I attack you, Meravyn will have to fight me."

Meravyn broke into a twisted grin. "I barely remember basic self-defense — but that really isn't the point, is it?"

I never meant to chain you, Jenchae thought at Elek. *I've failed. Failed you.* He didn't want to say those things; they flew out of his mind unbidden.

"You'll just have to live with that." Elek smiled. "Or die with it, I should say."

"Let him go," Meravyn repeated.

Jenchae eyed her. "Aren't you afraid?"

"I can't remember not being afraid. But that's the test of our fiber, isn't it? I lived with an HT for one hundred and thirty-seven years. I know the laws as well as any philosopher. He wants you to let him go, so you let him go. It's that simple. It's the rule without which a telepathic society cannot function. You know that."

~ • ~

The guard sprawled, and Akhté crumpled with him. Knees clacking on the floor, he doubled over, hands clutching his head. Jenchae stood stunned for two seconds? three? Then, his paralysis broke, and he rushed to Akhté. But Akhté was already staggering up. Ignoring Jenchae, he stepped over the corpse and planted the scrambler in the docking bay interface.

"No ships in for a while." He squeezed his eyes shut and rubbed his temples, exhaling a long, ragged breath. "Long enough for us to take our planet back." Then, he blinked and focused on Jenchae. "You're a good man, Jenchae. . ."

Jenchae could scarcely hear him. He was mesmerized by the trickle of blood from Akhté's nose.

As Akhté swayed and leaned back against the console, a footfall sounded in the doorway behind them.

Akhté looked up to face his brother. "I do what I must. Tell me, if you can, Dhri, that that is not the law of this life."

With a Mindtaxer's calm, his brother fired the gun.

Two days later, no Rha-Rhyd institution remained under Ash'torian control. It stayed a free and independent world for almost two years.

~ • ~

He could feel Akhté behind Elek's eyes.

"Yes, I'll do what I must," Jenchae said; a tiny smile of understanding flickered over Elek's face.

Jenchae made himself gaze into those eyes until they blurred and faded from his consciousness. Breaking the link between them was no different from severing any telepathic contact by reinstating mental blocks. But Jenchae had never before been so enmeshed in another person. Elek's thoughts chattered ceaselessly inside his own, as if someone in another room were talking too loudly.

Trying to cut out that noise was as hard as a child's first laborings at reading and blocking thoughts.

The process is the same, he told himself.

He imagined white walls ascending between them, enclosing him in a private whiteness. But the noise remained, Elek's mounting worry: *Don't you know how to do this?*

He turned away into himself, drowning out Elek, just as a boy with his fingers in his ears hums loud to pretend he can't hear his mother's scolding. He built up a white noise between Elek and himself, then waited, hearing only a sort of crackling. Now, he let that fade from his awareness, become the whistling of the ventilator his mind so seldom registered, till finally there was quiet inside, the stillness of solitude.

A wave of relief swept through Jenchae, and when he focused his eyes on Elek, the man appeared very far away. Elek heaved a sigh and squeezed his eyes shut a moment.

"I'm going to bed," he said. Trudging to the cot, he collapsed and was still.

CHAPTER THIRTEEN

Love and hate lie very close. They are, after all,
both effects of closeness.

Meravyn Sanston, personal letter to her sister (2100 A.E.)

Time sludges here, thought Meravyn.

Elek slept on, his cup and bowl untouched near the wall-
box.

Mechanically, Meravyn helped Jenchae eat.

Images fluttered before her: her cliff-shaded room in
Fivewells, the sun dancing poisonous on the plateau. Trenod's
gentle, boyish face. (Jenchae had told them that Akhté had
killed a man with his mind. Trenod could have done that. But,
no, he couldn't — because he could not have borne the pain.
And he was a better man than that.)

But she wasn't sure Jenchae was better. Clearly, at some
point, he had wrenched Elek's mind by force. For a sick
moment, she'd wondered if he'd enslaved Elek all this time. But
he hadn't. Elek had spoken of that forceful seizure as a separate
event. Probably Elek had attacked him. If so, Jenchae's reaction
was understandable. But not defensible.

She didn't want to be here, feeding Jenchae like an infant.
But Elek needed rest, and Jenchae's hands were broken. And the
duty to help others was the basis of civilized life.

Civilized life? Here? With nothing to look forward to
but death, did it matter?

Or was there still hope of escape? Maybe Ata. . .?

Her sister might be appealing her case. Meravyn
remembered her in a sky-blue robe, petting Nel on that last day.
Ata's mouth had turned hard when Meravyn explained she had

to go to Trenod's aid. "Thou thinks to prove he needs thee?
Thou won't."

Never needed me. I killed for him.

Now, we'll all die. All but Trenod. . .

But when?

Meravyn clacked Jenchae's spoon against his bowl too
loudly. She glanced at the cot, but Elek had not stirred.

"Jenchae," she said, "we've been here too long.
Wherever they were taking us, we should be there by now. It
makes me wonder if the ship is derelict and the meals
automated. We've been in here worrying about you and Elek
and not noticing how much time's gone by. Do you think
they've forgotten us?"

Jenchae was frowning at her. "You're right, Meravyn; I
haven't been thinking about it."

"There's too much to think about. It's like four or five
holo-programs playing different stories on top of each other.
Sometimes when I think of dying, it hurts as if a rib had
snapped. And then I think of you and Elek. And of me and
Manyrock and Tr — and whether there's any chance that I'll still
get a reprieve and whether our ship is lost somewhere and
whether I'll die at execution or of starvation here or of cold or
asphyxiation if life support goes — or if Elek will get us first."
She wondered as she spoke if he was awake, listening. "And
with all these types of dying, Jenchae, I still can't imagine that
I'm really going to die."

"They say no one alive can imagine dying."

"Can you?" *Have you been in the minds of the dying too?*

"Not really. Don't you want your rice?"

Meravyn took a mechanical bite. It stuck in her throat,
and she thought, *This is Jenchae's way of shutting me up.*

"I daydream it sometimes," he continued. "Not dying —
that will come soon enough — but death. I imagine what it
would be like to be in the realm of the Shonac gods or to bask in
the mind of Tra'hae. But that's just fancy, I expect. The realest it
ever seems is in those moments when I feel at peace, and there
are no regrets, no future, no me."

Meravyn had listened with her eyes on her bowl, turning it round. *Peace.* She was sick of the word. *Is there no rest from peace? No peace from peace? No peace? No peace, please.*

(His Akhté had been right about that.)

"Look, Jenchae," she said to change the subject. "There's an inscription on the bowl." It was carved along the rim in Ash'torian; it read: "Who can count the years of the universe Turning? Still less, who can count the Turns?"

She set bowl down, suddenly angry. "Why can't they leave us alone? Do they have to write their little 'wisdoms' on everything? They've condemned us to death; they might have the decency to let us spend our last hours in pea— without them."

Gingerly Jenchae scooped his own bowl out of her lap between his wrists. "Mine says, 'He who can take no other comfort can take comfort in mystery.'"

"Same thing. Everything's big and incomprehensible for them."

"Well, isn't it for us, too?" He smiled, wincing as he laid down his bowl.

Why does he have to do this? Why does he have to talk like this? No wonder Akhté left him.

"It doesn't matter," replied Meravyn. *And why do I keep indulging his talk?* "Life does not exist — or at any rate, life cannot perceive itself — in eternity. It understands only time, so why should we waste our time talking eternity?"

"That's what the 'mystery' quote means."

He is so pedantic!

"Then it's contradicting itself by insisting on talking eternity."

"Then so are you."

Meravyn hesitated. "So I am," she snapped. "And you could have the decency to let me, instead of trying to make us see everything with your eyes. Do you really believe that you have all the answers?"

"No, Meravyn. I'm sorry if I —"

"Oh, you're always sorry. You're never sorry. You invaded his mind!"

Jenchae gaped for a moment. "Yes. And now I've let it go."

"With enough coaxing."

He was nodding with a sort of reflexive agitation. "Very likely."

Part of Meravyn was all the angrier for his refusal to fight with her.

"I need to sleep," she said and settled facing the corner to the left of the door. Stretched on the unforgiving floor, she stared at the blacker lines that divided the tiles till they faded from her sight and the walls became nothing more than black and orange smudges.

~ • ~

Meravyn awoke to a scratching sound.

Rescue! she thought, then, *No. They've come to kill us.* She turned to see Elek scraping the last of the rice from his bowl.

Sleepy and a little dizzy, she pulled herself up to lean against the wall. Her neck ached, and her arm prickled where she'd been lying on it. Jenchae, she saw, was asleep on the opposite side of the floor.

Elek glanced at her and held up his bowl. "I've an inscription too. Would thou hear it?"

Meravyn almost told him not to read it. Instead, she sighed and held her tongue.

He read, "'Everyone is a messenger.'"

"That's all?"

"That's all."

She studied him. "Thou was awake when Jenchae and I were speaking?"

"Ye weren't speaking quietly. Thou specially. Thou was wrathful, Meravyn."

"I've enough to be wrathful for — as have we all."

A smile played around Elek's face. "Thou spoke kindly for me. I thank thee."

"'Twas wrong of him to take hold of thy mind."

"He knows it. But the second time, he did so at my bidding."

And now he's free, thought Meravyn. *Free to kill us.* But she couldn't make herself believe it enough to be afraid. He was toying absently with his spoon.

"Does thou fear dying?" she asked abruptly.

He hesitated. "Yea and nay."

"Which more: yea or nay?"

Again he was slow in answering. "I know not. I've other concerns more immediate."

"Killing?" said Meravyn brazenly.

"For one."

Meravyn forced back a catch in her throat. "We're fools to abandon ourselves here thus," she whispered, drawing closer to him.

"What would thou counsel?"

"We'd lose nothing to explore this cell once more for means of escape."

Elek shrugged and set down his bowl. "Explore thou the bed then," he said, "and I'll take the wall-box."

The moment Meravyn knelt by the cot, her heart sank. They wouldn't find anything. Still, dutifully, she probed its edges, listened for sounds from the other side of the alcove walls, ran her fingernails along the grooves between the tiles, under the thin bed mat. Nothing.

She turned to Elek, who had already moved on to investigating the door.

At her motion, he turned and hooked his thumb at the wall-box. "I fancy we've a possibility there — were we but a quarter our current size."

The joke annoyed Meravyn. But it set off a train of thought: "I wonder if they imprison small children here."

Elek was studying the door once more. "Doubtful. Retraining." He stood and sighed. "What else would thou have, Meravyn?" He glanced down as Jenchae stirred in his sleep.

Meravyn surveyed the cell. *The ceiling.* They had not examined it in detail in their previous search of the room, couldn't get high enough to look at it closely. Not unless one of them got a boost up from the other. The idea made Meravyn uneasy. Her better judgment told her to avoid physical contact, not to encourage the attraction of an emotionally unstable man.

130

But how could she justify letting squeamishness prevent her from checking every chance of escape?

"I'd have a closer look at the ceiling," she said. "Can thou lift me on thy shoulders?"

"I would say so," he answered, his tone comfortingly neutral.

Resolutely, Meravyn crossed to him and clambered up onto his back. They stumbled at it once, but then she was up, barely able to scrape the top of the cell with her fingertips. She focused on the ceiling, trying not to dwell on her thighs on his shoulders, his hands bracing her shins.

Precarious as she felt, the change of perspective was invigorating, almost like being in a different, higher room. Jenchae lay below small as a child. The ceiling itself glowed with phosphorescent patches, their texture identical to the rest of the cell's surface. The fresh air caressed her face; the ventilator hummed bee-like, but there was no mechanism to get behind, just tiny holes, a few per tile, scattered all over.

Cooling her fingertips on those rivulets of air, she leaned back too far and unsteadied Elek. As he staggered, she half-fell, half-slipped off his back, landing on her feet with a thud that echoed around the enclosure. They both looked at Jenchae, but he only twitched and sighed.

"He sleeps like a mountain, nay?" Elek whispered.

"He must be exhausted," Meravyn said, glad to be on her own feet again. "And thou too. Such mind-touch breeds fatigue."

Elek refused to meet her eyes. "So does this cell. Did thou find aught?" He nodded at the ceiling.

Meravyn shook her head. "I think I'll go mad in here."

Elek grinned. "If we shouted, thinks thou they'd hear us?"

"Nay. Or they'd ignore us."

Elek smiled a moment more.

"Let us out!" he cried in Ash'torian. The sound rebounded, throbbing in Meravyn's ears. Jenchae jerked up on his elbows.

Elek chuckled — and Meravyn found herself joining him, drowning out a twinge of guilt at Jenchae's slack-jawed staring.

"You won't, eh?" Elek addressed the ceiling. "You'll just pretend you can't hear us? So that means we can do anything in here. This is freedom; is that the point?" He waited a second or two. "So you wouldn't mind if we, say, threw a celebration?"

In one quick motion, he scooped his water cup from the floor, drained it, and lobbed it at Meravyn: "Catch."

Startled, she snatched it from the air and threw it back. It flew between them red as a smoldering coal, till Elek threw it too near to Jenchae. Meravyn missed it, and it clacked on the wall, just left of Jenchae.

Meravyn rushed to pick it up and set it by the wall-box. She was laughing as she hadn't in months, deep, desperate laughter that sucked at her chest. "That's just what we've been missing," she gasped. "Some good, rain-day fun."

On an impulse, she launched into a sand song in the old tongue, gratified that Elek joined her in the pounding, low-pitched chorus:

> *Hai! Il lusom ud dava,*
> *il lusom ud shíldava.*
> *Kelapúrli lore.*
> *Kelapúrli lore.*
> *purle oa'n' lusom,*
> *lusom ud shílavel,*
> *il kela vo dájasel,*
> *il kela vo eshtu n'atu.**

---

* The song is in Tral Keshnul, the dialect of the original sverra colonists on Manyrock.

Translation:
Oh, the sand in the sun,
The sand in the sunlight.
You make heat-dances.
You make heat-dances,
Heat, air, and sand,
Sand in the moonlight,
A dance of shadows,
A dance of gray and black.

Author's Note

They each sang a slightly different melody, jangling.
Impetuously, Meravyn held out her hand. With a spreading
grin, Elek grasped her arm, and they stomped a circle in the
traditional dance. As the song ended, they stopped and stood
breathing hard.

The room rang with a sudden hollowness.

"Will someone help me up?" said Jenchae.

Meravyn pulled him onto his feet, taking care to avoid
brushing his hands.

"Thanks." Jenchae shuffled past Elek and settled himself
on the cot with his back to them.

Meravyn wanted to feel sorry for him, but she couldn't
focus. Something between a remnant joy and a mounting
anxiety held her.

Elek was standing in the middle of the cell.

She said to him, "Thou sings the old Tral tongue well.
Was't native to thee?" He was old enough to have used it in his
youth rather than the Dab of the Sama colonists.

But he shook his head. "My mother was a Sama."

He slumped down by the wall opposite the wall-box.
After a moment, Meravyn joined him. If she had been free, she
would have gone away, gone home — the thought of home
pulled like a chain in her breastbone. Go home and get Nel from
Ata; how her poor dog must be pining for her, watching by the
window. But there was no way back. Here her choices were to
talk to her companions or ignore them, and she didn't want to
ignore him just now.

In standard Keshnul, the song would read:
Hah! Il luthom ud davlla,
Il luthom ud shíldavlla.
Krelapúrli lorey.
Krelapúrli lorey.
Purle oa'n' luthom,
Luthom ud shílavel,
Il krela po dájethal,
Il krela po eshlu n'atu.

Translator's Note

But she would rather be home.

Why had she left? She couldn't have left Trenod to the Ash'torians — but — could she? After all, wasn't he too high-profile for Ash'tor to do anything truly horrible to him? Couldn't she have let them arrest him, just for a while, and appealed to Leddra to intervene? But Leddra wouldn't have intervened, not between Ash'tor and an Ash'torian citizen. She'd thought of all these possibilities before she'd left Manyrock. It wasn't as if she was a fool.

But Trenod might have spoken for her at her trial. He might have sent a statement at any rate. Perhaps he had tried, and they'd disallowed it, but. . .

The pain welled up into halting words. "I think that thou was not entirely wrong in those things thou said about Trenod."

Elek's eyes flashed on her too bright.

"Thou was wrong to judge him so hard," she added. "But 'tis true. . . 'tis true I'd not expect him to walk right across the Lus for me. He lives for himself first. But then, do not we all?" She tried to smile, failed.

"Not thou. Thou lives and dies for him."

"Thou seems to know a great lot about me."

He looked down at his bowl. "I know thy sort."

She scoffed. "Yea? And what is my sort then?"

He took a deep breath. "Thou's one of those who cast away their lives for the love of one who would never do the like for them."

"My life is not cast away."

"Is it not so? Here I fancied thou was bound for execution."

The thought was not new, and Meravyn had her answer ready. "I have lived a hundred nine-and-sixty years, and one thing only has stopped me living exactly as I pleased: 'tis Ash'tor, not my husband. To risk myself for him at the last was not to cast away my life but to live as I have chosen."

"Yea, and every word thou says, thou proves my point the more."

"Has thou no conception of love at all?" she whispered. "Can thou truly not comprehend sacrificing thyself to spare thy love from torment?"

Elek stared motionlessly ahead.

At length, he said, "Yea, I've a conception of love." For several seconds, he was silent. Then he met her eyes. "I've known what it is to love one who loves another. I know it well enough to know the feeling when it looms up."

Meravyn's chest contracted. "Thou says that as if *I've* done something amiss."

He shook his head, then buried it in his hands.

And it seemed to Meravyn she knew exactly what that meant: *Life heaps trials with no regard for how much we can hold without buckling.*

With a rush of emotion, she put an arm around his shoulder. He started, looking up at her warily. Unsure what she ought to do, fearing it was a mistake, Meravyn drew him closer — and closer, until their foreheads touched, and then their lips.

Together, they pulled away.

He sighed. "Thou's too like to her."

"Like to whom?"

He looked away. "Ned'yem."

"Ash'torian?"

"Yea. I've no apology for it. Her life-sharer — he was everything to her. That thou understands. After he was killed, she joined a mercenary group I was a party to. She lived as if her life were over. When she came to me, she said 'twas from loneliness only. I said I understood. But she injured me, her distance did. One day, I killed her." The drone of his voice ceased like a recording switched off.

For a moment, Meravyn was too afraid to move. After some seconds, she collected herself enough to say with some semblance of calm, "Thou wishes to kill me?"

"If I wished to kill thee, thou would be dead."

He rose, his eyes on the cot. Following his gaze, Meravyn could see Jenchae staring at them over his shoulder.

Elek glanced back at Meravyn. "Excuse me," he said with a restrained civility he had never used before. Then, he went into the lav and stayed there.

~ • ~

Now Jenchae was looking at Meravyn. She turned away from his gaze. After some seconds, she heard a swish of fabric.

A quick glance told her he'd lain back again on the cot. Meravyn let out a breath she hadn't realized she'd been holding. She didn't want to talk to Jenchae, didn't want his advice or his sympathy or questions.

She wanted to hide, to escape. Sitting in the corner by the entrance, as far from the cot and the lav as she could get, she had an image of throwing herself at the door and wrenching it open with hysterical strength.

Before, Elek's rages had been held in check by Jenchae, and resenting Jenchae for that mental invasion, he had directed his anger toward him — and Meravyn had come to feel almost safe; she, after all, was the one he liked.

But now Jenchae had lost his hold. And as for Meravyn — oh, Elek did like her. He liked her just like a woman he'd murdered.

Once Meravyn had had a friend who'd been infatuated with her. He'd accepted that she couldn't reciprocate. Yet simply knowing how he'd cared for her had made her uncomfortable with him. Her feeling for Elek was that former discomfort expanded to terror.

With Elek, she was powerless. Her very being, the characteristics that made her herself, inflamed him. She had no way of knowing when she might send his rage surging. She shouldn't mention Trenod, of course, but he already knew what Trenod was to her. If she looked wistful in the wrong way, would he. . .?

She tried to steel herself. Of course, she wasn't powerless. And she must be prepared to defend herself. Ned'yem had been a human, but she was a Tral, and her raw physical strength was in the region of his own. And she *had* studied physical defense once long ago. She would review it in her mind, practice what she could in the lav. And there was Jenchae: he would do his best to help her. Maybe he could seize Elek's mind again.

No. No, that was not an option. To think it was hypocrisy.

But at least, Jenchae could physically get in Elek's way, hamper him enough for her to get a good blow in. Together, perhaps, they could kill him.

The thought sent a shudder through her.

Was life worth so much — to kill a man with one's bare hands to gain a few days or few hours more life?

But she would do it if she had to, and knowing that steadied her.

With what detachment she could muster, she asked herself if he would try to rape her. She told herself she didn't think so. The way he had described his rage, it seemed briefer than that — a burst of a few moments only. Perhaps that was a good sign. Perhaps if she could simply hold him off for a time, the rage would wear out on its own.

Because he didn't want to kill her. He'd ensconced himself in the lav because he didn't want to.

A wave of pity passed through her and in its wake, relief like rain. He wasn't her enemy.

What a waste his life had been! There was good in him: he loved the trees, sang the old songs. Underneath the anger, he cared about Jenchae — that had been plain when he'd helped him to eat. What was it that had gone wrong in him?

It was the question Jenchae had asked of Akhté, and the answer was every bit as elusive for Elek as for Jenchae's friend — more so, because she knew nothing really of Elek's past, except that he was forged in the brutal frontier days of Shinegray. She wanted to know more of him. To make him comprehensible would make him less terrifying.

Yet that way, perhaps, lay nothing but another invasion.

CHAPTER FOURTEEN

And 'Medhebaq* said unto his brother, "Brother, I forgive you your betrayal. I hold that it is washed away as the dust upon the river." But 'Sylseq answered, "Brother, it comes not within the bounds of your grace to forgive me. Tra'hae himself will not wash clean the stain of the betrayer in this Turn."

"The Shadow Poem of Yor," *Retellings of the Nine Clans* (c. 200 B.E.)

Elek scrunched in the corner of the lav, his toe touching the base of the toilet. He wound his arms tight around his shins, pushed his face hard against his knees. He hoped he could vent the violence that way, by forcing his strength down onto his own body. This wasn't the rage, he knew at once, but its cousin. Not anger. He wasn't angry at her. That would come later. It would come in a heartbeat. It would stalk him and spring like a cat in the night.

This — this was simply overload. This was safer, he reminded himself. Yes, this, for the moment, was safe, and he didn't need Jenchae. He would not turn to Jenchae again.

In some corner of himself, there was relief that Jenchae wasn't sharing this. Now Elek's thoughts and his pains and his rage were his own.

But Meravyn... Why did she have to be so much like *her*? Why did she have to bring him back to that last day?

---

* 'Medhebaq Khe'byq Yor was the founder of the Clan Yor.

Translator's Note

138

The Ash'torians had paused in their incursions. An uprising on Yorûn had diverted their attention, and they'd left only a few personnel on Besqûn ensconced in collaborators' fortresses. And so the Core leaders had been giving out leaves.

It was the afternoon of the last day of Elek and Ned'yem's holiday at the Arches of Eba. In the evening, they would break their camp in the caves and wait for Dasho to fetch them. For now, Ned'yem, in a UV suit, was up on a ledge, running a gloved hand across one of the massive stone arches long ago eroded out of the surrounding sandstone. Elek was exploring the tiny cacti in the rock cracks, tinier ants running over their spines. As he glanced up, his eye fell on her, her suit silvery against the dusty rock and the bright blue autumn sky. The rains had swept through late in the night, washing in one of those transparent days when each color and shape leaps out as exact as a computerized illusion.

Elek climbed up on the ledge beside her and tried to unravel what she saw in the rock. It was volcanic, pockmarked by ancient lava bubbles and gleaming with mineral lines.

"There's something written here," said Ned'yem, "in the language only Tra'hae can speak." She ran her fingers over the rock's rough surface. "It reminds me of the writings engraved on the walls of Lane'bib City. Am I right to think you haven't been there?" She spared him a quick look.

"No, I've never been on Lane'bib."

"There, one is hard-pressed to find a stone that has not been etched with words. The record of the ages underfoot." She paused. "I met him on Lane'bib."

She had not spoken of Hahbah'mah for over a month. She'd been happier, her eyes questing out the beauties of Besqûn. They had explored the mountains and plains together, counting up beetle species, wondering at flowers flinging out mutant whorls of petals. But now these Besqûnian rocks were speaking to her of *him* again. Perhaps they had never ceased.

For a moment Elek hated him. For dying, for living, for yammering in the rock in "the language only Tra'hae can speak" — as if he were God. And deeper, he was simmering at

Ned'yem, who couldn't get her brain around the simple fact that obsession with death makes life impossible.

You need to snap out of it, he thought in Dab, but he said in Ash'torian, "Neyda, sooner or later, we have to let the dead be dead."

She turned to him, her expression glassed over by the UV shielding of her faceplate. "You're right, of course." She hesitated. "I was thinking — not just of him — but of all the ancient wisdoms that admonish us to value the present moment." She caressed the corrugated stone as she spoke. "They teach that what matters most is what we live and feel, what is here, here and now."

"It's true," said Elek.

"But it is not absolutely true. Because without regard for past or future, there is no loyalty, no progress, no will to change." She fell silent some moments. "I don't know how to weigh these things."

Elek gripped the shoulder of her suit with a gloved hand. "Let's go back into the cave and take off these suits for a while."

They spent the rest of the afternoon behind the UV screen they'd brought to block the cave's mouth. Reclining on their sleeping mat, they looked out at the panorama of the Eba Plateau shifting through the hours. They talked of things, but later on, Elek would not remember what. What crystallized in his memory was the blue sky over streaks of yellow-red rock and earth — and the cave, marking a meridian between day and night, balmy at its sun-drenched entrance and shadow-cold behind. And Neyda's hand in his own, small and hot and slippery with sweat. He thought of what she said about living in the present. He thought, *Yes, this is why one lives.*

At some point, while the shadows of the arches lengthened into hemispheric trenches on the ground, Elek slept.

He awoke to a warm evening breeze on his face. From the mouth of the cave, the land glowed rose beneath an indigo sky. She had switched off the UV shield as the sun sank. She was no longer in the cave. He yawned, stretched, and ventured out to find her.

It did not take him long to spot her. She was on her knees by one of the minor arches facing away from him into a

140

sunset spread like blood on the horizon. He had thought that then: *the sky is blood.* Had he thought it before or after he saw the blood on the earth?

As in a dream, he floated toward her.

She knelt with her arms flung wide as wings, her hair redder than her russet clothes, red as the sunset, and yet less red than the blood that flowed down her arm to blacken in the dust, blood from the fresh gouge she had opened over the grieving scar she had made for Hahbah'mah.

Elek had no words for the hatred he felt for her. To her, all he had given meant nothing: all the hours that he'd listened as she spoke of *him*, all the words of comfort he had summoned up, all the times she had lain in his arms and professed her devotion to someone else. No, not even to someone else: to a ghost, a memory. And all that time Elek had been by her side, and she had refused to see him. Even now, as his feet thumped up behind her, she could not tell he was there. Or didn't care to stir.

But this time she would see him.

He pulled her up by her bleeding arm and jerked her around to face him. Her eyes were wide with surprise. Not love, not understanding, not even remorse, not even enough respect to realize she should fear him.

"It is not enough!" he snarled. She must be made to see. In a fluid motion, he dropped her arm, seized her throat, and smashed her head into the stone arch. The feel of her skull cracking open sent a shock of relief through his body. The satisfaction of justice. He held her there a moment, but her swelling eyes were not on him.

Then she fell at his feet, her head a bloody pulp. She gurgled a little as the seconds stretched like rubber. And then she was still.

His mind ceased working.

She deserved —

But she didn't. And he loved her. But then how. . .?

His legs gave out and he collapsed on his knees beside her, couldn't look at her, looked out instead at the deepening dark of the sky, fading to a dried-blood brown.

~•~

The last afterglow of the sun had faded when a white light flared over him. A sudden wind flurried the dust on all sides. A thrumming engine stilled.

Some time passed before he heard Dasho's voice, quiet: "I didn't think you'd have the fortitude."

Fortitude? He couldn't speak.

"I know you cared about her," Dasho went on after a moment. "At least you seemed to." A pause. "Were you playing her from the beginning?"

Playing? Still he could not answer a word.

At length, Dasho added, "We should have known an Ash'torian wouldn't really join us."

Elek heard himself say, "No. You never pry the Raptured away from the Raptured." Slowly, his survival instinct was winding up for action. "How did you find out?" he asked Dasho, testing, still looking out onto the black horizon.

"Just got the word from the Second Admin. I guess they'd been checking up on her a long time, finally excavated her records. Guess they told you first."

"Just enough," said Elek. "You tell me the rest."

He could hear Dasho sigh and crouch behind him. "Doubt I know much more than you do. She was an infiltrator back on Manyrock; then, she got assigned here to break Core. Seems she really did have old college friends here, Besqûnians who'd trust her, let her get in close. Bet they're reeling."

The blood was pounding in Elek's ears, his legs too weak to stand on.

She sighed. "Should have known no Rapt's a friend to any but a Rapt."

"The assassination?"

"Of the Manyrock ambassador?"

"Part of her plan?"

"Who can say?" said Dasho. "But she didn't do it anyway — break Core yet. She was still gathering information." A silence. "You got her in good time."

A spy. She'd been a spy.

Elek had got what he needed from Dasho. With that grudging strength that only came because it must, he stood up and crossed to her ship, leaving Dasho to dispose of Ned'yem in whatever way she saw fit.

~ • ~

He couldn't stay with Core, of course. Not on account of the wary looks or the wide berth they gave him in the hall. They had already known he was a brutal fighter. Brutality wasn't necessarily bad when disposing of a spy. They were more careful around him now; that was all.

No, he couldn't stay because he had to go to Manyrock, to look at her files. He had to find out just how far she'd betrayed him. Core was happy enough to see him go, to hook him into their Manyrock spy network. After all, he ought to be of use as a spy on his native planet.

He made a poor spy though. There was something in his manner that made him stand out, made people who had only seen him once remember his face. He wasn't certain why he had that effect, only that it was more apparent since Ned'yem's death. But he went through the motions of helping the network and managed to finagle access to the files they'd collected on her.

She had apparently really come from R'Ebsyn, really worked as a simultaneous translator. Her previous experience as a spy was uncertain. It was only clear that she had received orders to infiltrate Besqûn. She was to be hired as a translator by the Ash'torian Embassy and contrive to leak specified information to Core through a contact she'd made on Manyrock, one who would be inclined to trust her. Once Core believed her to be an Ash'torian double agent, she would begin to gather information on their organization for referral to Ash'tor.

But the strategy had not gone as planned. Instead, she had arrived as a refugee on Besqûn at a remote port outside the Ash'torian sphere of influence and thrown herself on the mercy of old friends there, pleading sympathy for the Besqûnians' cause.

It seemed that this much of her story had been real: when Hahbah'mah had been killed, she had, in fact, missed her scheduled ship and taken alternate transport to Besqûn. And as for Hahbah'mah, he was apparently truly her life-sharer. Her records listed him as a close personal acquaintance. He was not mentioned in connection with any of her official duties.

~ • ~

It was the first night Elek hadn't had to work since returning to Manyrock, a winter night that had fallen swiftly while he read through Ned'yem's files. Finished reading, he left the stuffy heat of his room and walked into the light of the two new-risen moons. Being on the outskirts of the capital of Songport, he only needed to walk ten minutes to be out onto the crunching gravel of the plains.

The breeze, whispering cool past his face, carried a familiar dusty scent. The mountains gloomed dark in the distance, speckled with glowing settlements. It was calming here. But it didn't help him make sense of Ned'yem.

So she had loved Hahbah'mah as she'd claimed? She'd told the truth about that even through lies about everything else? Lies about him? She was a liar, a traitor — an oppressor. Loyal to *them*. She'd deserved to die. That was his function — his place in the universe — to kill the oppressors.

But he hadn't known she was with them when he'd turned on her. He had simply killed her, as he'd killed his friend in the marula grove. And others who had not been oppressors either. He used to feel guilty about it. If he had any remorse at all, it ought to be for Ned'yem, whom he'd loved. Yes, he was quite sure he'd loved her.

But he couldn't feel anything now. Surely, he should feel something. Sorrow. He'd had no right to kill her. She'd had no right to lie, to betray him. But he had lied too, lied when he'd claimed he wanted nothing but to help her. No, whatever she'd done, he'd had no right to kill her. Yet she'd had no right to live.

It occurred to him that there were no rights at all, only actions, only survival or death. Pain or the momentary absence of pain. And feeling always tended toward pain in the end; therefore, it was wisest to feel nothing. Remorse accomplished nothing. Love accomplished nothing. Looking for patterns within the chaos only occasioned more distress.

He listened to his feet scratching over the gravel. Listen and live, second by second.

The rest was not worth his time or trouble. Not again.

~ • ~

But now it was crashing in. Jenchae had done this, slipped into his mind and stirred things. Meravyn had done this, going on and on and on about her Trenod. Elek had done it to himself. He had killed Ned'yem — a precious living being and he'd killed her. He was the murderer, no one else. And if any of them had betrayed him, his betrayal was a thousand times worse.

He pressed his face against his knees so hard he could see lights flash in front of his closed eyelids. Tears squeezed out and ran down his nose. His muscles trembled with fatigue, but it would not be enough to stop the rage when it came. Because it was never enough.

He would kill them. Meravyn was strong but not strong enough, not brutal enough. Jenchae would not stop him. Jenchae would keep his word never to take hold of Elek's mind again. Even if Elek begged Jenchae to seize his brain if he started to attack, Jenchae would be too craven to do it, too afraid of ending up like Akhté. Because, in Jenchae's mind, it was Jenchae himself, not Elek, who was the true reflection of Akhté. Elek could see that clearly, even without their minds connected.

So there was no help. He would kill them both the moment the hatred came. Perhaps he should just stay here in the lav — but he couldn't. Sooner or later, one of them would evict him. Perhaps that would be the instant, the trigger.

Jenchae had wanted to teach him control. Mindtaxing exercises? Elek had tried them many times in his life.

But that was before Jenchae. Jenchae had changed him — for better? for worse? He couldn't tell.

Could it make a difference, if he did his best to practice Jenchae's techniques right now? Could it save him, at least, in these final hours before the Quol'shab took all the struggle away?

He drew in a shuddering breath. Like some rusted machine, he unwound his arms and staggered to his feet. With decision, he opened the door and confronted the two sets of eyes locked on him.

They had no right to stare like that. But Elek swallowed his indignation.

"Jenchae," he said. "Teach me your Mindtaxing tricks."

CHAPTER FIFTEEN

The antonym of "peace" is "war." But the
antonym of "peace" is also "striving."

Fundamental Precepts of Dwo explicated by Jûz
Lagadágaw (281 B.E.)

It was counter to nature to try to think of nothing. And
Elek had been round this mountain before. He already knew
how to do all these things: controlled breathing, blanking his
thoughts. Decades he'd practiced them — and they helped a
little but not enough. Relearning them now was pointless.

"You are so far from tranquil you might as well be in a
shouting match," said Jenchae.

Elek wanted to smack him. As if he needed Jenchae to
tell him how raw he was now. He snapped his eyes open to see
the man sitting a meter in front of him. Clenching his fist, Elek
tried to keep his voice light: "Looking into my mind again, eh?"

Jenchae stared at him too searchingly. At least, there was
no chatter from Jenchae's brain. "I can sense a trace of your
emotions now, like I can with most people. That's a good thing,
by the way, much more normal than when we first met. But I
hardly need that to see you're agitated."

"Congratulations."

He felt as if a stimulant were swimming in his blood.

"So what can I do?" asked Elek, trying to sound calm.

"We could keep practicing until it comes to you, the
peacefulness."

Elek smiled. "Or until I tear your arms off. Whichever
comes first."

Jenchae took a deep breath. "Or you could look into my mind, see if you can make use of my abilities, without my enforcing them on you."

Elek's first instinct was to scream. Entangle their minds again! Now! When they'd only just got free!

What possible good —?

Elek froze and commanded his voice to stay even: "What would be the point of trying that now if you couldn't show me before?"

"Before, I was overwhelmed by your thoughts. It was all I could do to clamp down on your rage. Now I'm myself again." He paused as if reflecting. "I can show you the peace within myself. Such as it is."

Did that make sense?

"I wouldn't be doing anything to you," Jenchae added, "just letting you see me."

It felt false, too easy. "Now? Why not in the beginning? You could have saved us both so much. . ." He broke off.

"Your mind was closed then. You couldn't reach me."

If it kept them safe, kept Meravyn safe. . .

She was sitting in the corner by the door, stock still.

Elek's nails dug into his flesh. He forced his fist to unclench — it was a good sign that he could still make it obey him. After some seconds, his hand relaxed, the only part of him that did.

Jenchae was looking at him coolly, as if Elek's struggle could not touch him. Of course, it couldn't; Jenchae had freed his mind of it. Yet Jenchae was offering to open himself to that turmoil again. He was crazy.

But perhaps it was the wisest course.

"All right," said Elek. "I'll look at your mind."

He took a breath and concentrated on lowing his blocks, just as he would fix his eyes on a dark spot far off in the desert. He couldn't count the years since he'd tried to reach another's thoughts that way.

And yet — remarkably — it was easy, perhaps because of the bond they'd shared. Easy to feel that familiar presence, not deeply but softly, like a cool stream. All at once, he understood the reason behind the ritual breathing, the visualizations. It was a quiescence, a deep half-conscious rest. He pictured the stream — or perhaps it was Jenchae who pictured it — and slipped along it as lightly as the leaves of a water plant.

~ • ~

For the first time since her arrest, Meravyn slept soundly. Whatever Jenchae had shown Elek, it worked. He was calm. He would sit with closed eyes, breathing almost as if he'd been asleep, but he wasn't. He was turning inward, finding the stillness in himself.

At first she wondered if he was just going through the motions. But it looked real, and Jenchae assured her it was. Without willing it, she felt herself safe again — safe enough to let sleep steal over her; she even had use of the cot for several hours.

How long went by that way? More than a day. Four meals' worth of little but sleeping punctuated by eating. Meravyn was increasingly convinced that something was wrong on board the ship; otherwise, they would have reached their destination. But for a few hours, she was too tired to care.

The first time she awoke truly refreshed, she saw Elek sitting in the corner to the right of the door; he was facing her, staring somewhere over her head. She got up from the cot and sat on the floor, watching. Jenchae was asleep on the opposite side of the door from Elek. Could Elek access the calm of Jenchae's mind when he was asleep?

If Elek was aware of her, he made no sign, and so she went on watching him careless of her rudeness.

It seemed wrong all of a sudden: to eat and sleep and watch — and do nothing and say nothing when, one way or another, these were her last hours of life. There ought to be more meaning. She shuddered.

Elek's gaze snapped onto her. "Are you all right, Meravyn?" he asked quietly. And in Ash'torian too — well, probably that was for the best.

She scooted toward him with heavy limbs. She didn't want to be near him, but she wasn't going to talk across the room at him when Jenchae was trying to sleep.

About a meter away, she stopped and said, "I'm all right. And you?"

He nodded. "It's not so bad."

"Is there anything I can do? Or should I keep my distance?"

He watched her for a moment. "I didn't mean to frighten you, talking about Ned'yem."

"Yes, you did. But you were right to warn me."

He shook his head. "Small good a warning would do in here. We'll all be dead soon anyway. Is it really worth fearing?"

Meravyn laughed under her breath. "I've been asking myself the same thing."

He smiled and let his gaze slip away.

Meravyn sat by him a long time, afraid — but not of him.

~•~

I lied to him. Jenchae had invited Elek to look into his thoughts and share his techniques for stilling the mind. And Elek had done so — and benefited from it but not in the way Jenchae had promised. Elek had not, in fact, learned a technique Jenchae used, not any standard Mindtaxer's technique. Rather, Jenchae had designed a trigger commanding him to fall passive when agitated. Almost a hypnotic suggestion. That wasn't what Elek had wanted, but it was the only thing that Jenchae had to give. And if it protected Meravyn and himself — and Elek, too, from his own horror of their deaths — wasn't that serving all of them?

But if his act was justified, why was he afraid to tell Elek the truth? One answer was plain: to know the truth would break his calm; it would make him resist. He would consider it another manipulation. And he would, of course, be correct.

Jenchae watched Elek sleep on the cot.

"You look grim." Meravyn seated herself on the floor beside him.

"Tired. Wishing I knew when this would be over."

"Are you sharing my thoughts now?" Meravyn smiled. "I'm glad, at least, I'm not alone."

Jenchae sighed, looking back at Elek. "I never meant to take his mind over."

Meravyn was silent for a moment. "Yet perhaps he needed that impetus to be able to change himself at all."

150

"Maybe. His mind was very silent." He shook his head. "Wasted time, that's what I can't help feeling. Our seconds clicking down, and we've lost so much time fighting."

Meravyn leaned against the wall and sighed. "It reminds me of the history of Manyrock, maybe history in general. On Manyrock, we spent so much time squabbling among ourselves. 'Ourselves' — I can call us that now, the Trals and the Samas together. We could have been fortifying our planet, our culture, so that we'd be strong enough to resist Ash'tor. Instead we squabbled. In the northlands two hundred years ago, the Samas slaughtered Trals by the hundred; did you know that?"

"It happens," said Jenchae. It all seemed unimportant here. He had given Elek rest, and soon they would all be given over to the great and final rest. What now could be worth bothering over? "Violence, it seems, always comes around in the cycle," he commented absently.

"The Trals oppressed the Samas too," put in Elek, gazing across the room at them.

"Certainly," said Meravyn, "but not with the same concerted effort."

"Sometimes with very concerted effort," said Elek. Jenchae could hear the catch in the words, yet the calm remained, eerie — breaths floating like an owl upon fog.

"Where are you thinking of?" Meravyn asked.

"Shinegray, when I was young."

Jenchae stifled a nervous quiver. *Can — should — this false peace float him through whatever memories he held of that?*

CHAPTER SIXTEEN

> It is rumored that the Kiri Nation engineered the
> Trals as a superior species to govern a flawed
> humanity. It is to the credit of the Trals that they
> have not risen to that challenge more often.
>
> Minister Meeden Zasha, public address on the
> Truce of Manyrock States
> (1873 A.E.)

Elek's mother was sitting on her mat in the cool corner of their room, her knees drawn up and her forehead pressed upon them. Her short auburn hair was hiding her face.

"Bren," he said. He always called her by her name in the Sama way, while the Tral children called their parents, "Mother" and "Father." It marked him as a Sama slave, but it wasn't the only thing that marked him, and it was the way she'd taught him, so he did it. "Bren, Lan Jelna* met me in the path and said I should send thee to her." Lan Jelna was their house-overseer†, a

---

* Lan: an honorific in Tral Keshnul. In standard Keshnul, it signifies the distinction, "the only one."

Translator's Note

† In the town of Shinegray at this period, the Sama slaves were held collectively as the property of the Tral community but each Sama was under the direct authority of a house-overseer, who saw to their material needs, and a work-overseer, who enforced their labor. The overseers were accountable to the Tral community at large.

Author's Note

tall, stately Tral, black as obsidian with flashing eyes and flashing teeth. She wasn't a cruel one, but that didn't stop Elek's heart from pounding when she spoke to him.

Bren raised her head. Lan Jelna had demanded she have half the day off for an abortion, the third that Elek could remember — but he was only eleven, and he wondered sometimes how many others there had been. They always left Bren looking tired and blank.

"Take a bath, Elek," she said. "Thou smells like the sewage plant. There's a fresh allotment of cleanser by the basin." She got to her feet, pulled on her sun cloak, and disappeared out the door.

That was a good day. It wasn't usual to allot more than the bare necessities to slaves, but Lan Jelna decided that contraception had become a necessity for Bren. She argued that Bren would work better if she were sterilized and got the village committee to agree.

That evening, Bren smiled as they sat on the mat and drank their water.

"Thou's lucky thou's a hybrid, Elek."

"Why so?" he asked sullenly, "They hate hybrids most."

It was true. At first, the Trals had thought hybrids would mean stronger slaves. But what they meant chiefly was more fights among the Sama and hybrid children and stronger bodies to revolt. And strength wasn't what they needed anyway. The dirty jobs were just dirty, not heavy. There were only three hybrids in Shinegray now and everyone hated them. They even learned to hate each other — every time they'd been seen together, they'd been beaten for plotting. Better not to seek each other.

"Thou's lucky," his mother said, "that thou's naturally sterile. 'Twould mean more to thee if thou were a girl, but still thou can be thankful."

"I've heard tales that in the South some hybrids have had hybrid children."

Bren shrugged. "It may be. Myself, I've heard tales that parents there can do things with genes that will make their children fertile. Why they should wish to, I cannot guess."

~•~

"By the time I was born," said Elek, "Shinegray had been populated for a long time by a semi-nomadic Tral community. One year, they came back to their winter grounds and found that a Sama ship had landed and set up a village." He laughed a little; he wasn't sure why. "The Trals weren't pleased. The Samas were poorly fortified, so it didn't take long for the Trals to put them down. Some wanted all the Samas killed; others didn't. They ended up keeping the Samas as an underclass, using the ship's machinery and the humans' labor to set up a permanent town."

"They were badly treated?" said Jenchae.

Elek thought a moment, surprised by the calm in his mind. "I suppose we weren't treated very well."

~ • ~

Bren laid a towel doused in cleanser across Elek's shoulders. It was to soothe his cuts, not keep him clean, but the cleanser was cool and came cheaper than water. He was glad he was facing away from her; he didn't want her to see how red his eyes were. At thirteen, he ought to be too old to cry. He was glad she didn't chide him. She almost never chided him anymore for getting punished. The punishment was punishment enough, he guessed.

It wasn't his fault. This time that boy, Davu, had gone too far. Elek was tired of being told how he was inferior to a real Sama just because the smells of the sewage plant bothered him more, when, if anything, he was superior to those Samas. He could have crushed Davu with a single blow. But he didn't. He'd only hit him hard enough to break his jaw; they could fix that up. And Davu had deserved it, after all.

But, of course, Lan Evlar hadn't seen it that way. The work-overseer had dragged him out to the retraining room and beaten him until he'd knocked Elek's head on the floor and Elek gone unconscious. He was better off than Davu, though, he thought with pride. He was hard to really hurt; he was strong like a Tral that way.

At least Lan Evlar hadn't used him for sex today. For about a year, he'd been a target of the work-overseer, but probably today he had smelled too much like the plant. Of course, given a choice between the sex and a beating, he would

154

choose the sex without hesitation. It hurt far less. But a beating was preferable to both together.

"'Tis the gods," said Bren from behind him.

Elek looked up at the stars over the mountaintop and had a confused idea that the gods were up there, living on the other worlds, the better worlds where there were just Samas.

No place for him.

"What's the gods?" he asked.

"The madness. They tell that the gods are mad and that their madness festers in the hearts of all folk who hear their voices — without knowing that they've heard aught."

Elek felt a surge of pity for Bren — and anger for Davu — and Lan Evlar too. How dare they accuse him of being too violent? Him! Wasn't he always good to Bren?

True, when he was four or five, he had thrown a tantrum and pushed Bren hard across the room. She'd slipped and slammed into the wall and had the breath knocked out of her. She'd gasped and gasped, and he'd been so afraid. She was a little woman; she was weak even for a Sama, but he'd learned that day to be gentle with her. And wasn't he always? Didn't he carry her from her mat to the toilet when she was ill?

How could they call him a violent boy? Apashar didn't, the Sama boy who liked him. Apashar said he was better in bed than a real Tral, that he wasn't so heavy and that he acted nice. He *was* nice — to people who were nice to him. Who had the right to ask more than that?

The crickets were sounding in the cracks by the path.

"Are all the gods mad?" he asked his mother.

She pointed a finger over his shoulder to the heavens. "Sees thou that star rising over Twoteeth Peak? And the two above and the faint one to the right? Before the war, in the great days of the empire, the ancients named that constellation the Seat of Elidairos, Lord of Reason, the only one of the gods not mad. This world, then, was held to lie under his protection. 'Twas a haven world to sing to the gods. Yea, one could sing to them and comfort them, nor be touched by their madness. Thus did they call this world Tsoürn, the Singing World, where the voice of Reason sang in the wind-whisper of the trees." She let her hand drop. "Now this world too is mad. 'Tis funny, is it not?"

Elek tried to find it funny but without success.

~•~

"My mother and I were in service to the Trals at Shinegray till I was fourteen," Elek paused.

After a moment, Meravyn asked, "What happened then?"

"Somehow — I don't know exactly — the Samas from Tenstar Ridge found out there were Sama slaves in Shinegray. They attacked the town and freed them."

Meravyn's mouth was a thin, bloodless line, her eyes narrowing as he spoke. Like all Manyrockers, she'd heard about the Samas of Tenstar.

"They massacred the Trals," she said, half-question, half-statement.

"I'd like to tell you I was sorry, Meravyn, but I really wasn't."

~•~

Elek and Bren watched in weird fascination the dust clouds on the trail above. Out of the clouds issued voices rebounding off the mountainsides in Keshnul and Dab, cries and the sound of guns. They could hear the pounding of footsteps now, vague figures descending out of the dust.

"'Tis more than could be hoped," breathed Bren.

Up the trail, a Tral fell beneath a Sama nerve gun; he writhed, casting up fresh dust clouds while the Sama hollered curses.

Elek jumped at the touch of Bren's hand on his arm. Her eyes were stark with a new understanding. "By hell, Elek, thou must flee. Now, lest they think thee a Tral."

"Bren —"

"Now! Thou has no time."

"Where?"

"Anywhere. Far from them." She pushed at him; it scarcely moved him, and yet she had pushed him with all of her strength. "Go!" she shouted. And he ran.

Half-unconsciously, he followed the route he'd taken once when at six or seven, he'd tried to run away. He ran from the dust clouds, skipping faster than he'd dreamed he could down into boulder country, the evening sun casting treacherous streaks of white on black over jagged stones. Finally, he reached the place, a crevice amid the boulders, almost too small now for him to fit into. But not quite. He lay still and tried to listen over the sound of his own ragged breathing.

He could still hear screaming, sometimes nearer, sometimes far. The sun sank and the twilight breeze batted his face. He wondered if Samas would hurt any other Samas. Would they hurt Bren if they found out that she was his mother? And what would they do to him? And what would he do if he couldn't go back, out here without even his sun-cloak, without water?

He cried for a while, cursing himself for the water waste.

He would have to go back, for supplies if nothing else.

All three moons were out that night. None full, yet together they cast enough light to paint a world of silver — or was it black and white as Trals came in black and white? Real Trals, who didn't have brown human hair like their mothers'.

When it had been quiet for perhaps an hour, Elek crept out from the rocks and padded back toward Bren's hut. It was on the outskirts of the village, a periphery usually guarded. Perhaps it was guarded tonight as well — by different guards. Elek knew only that he did not see one. Almost crawling, he made for the light in his mother's amber-tinted window. Close by, he could hear voices inside: a man's voice and Bren's. He peered over the sill.

She seemed unharmed. She was sitting on her mat, talking with a Sama man seated on the floor a meter or two away.

"Ye see my meaning, then?" the man was asking.

"Yea," said Bren. "There is no question, 'twere better he had not been born."

"If he died with the rest here, 'twould be a mercy."

Bren inclined her head. "A kind of mercy."

Elek's heart crumpled inside him. A mercy? His death? No, she could not mean that. She could not mean she wished him dead. He was her only child; they were everything to each other. It was a trick. It had to be. But what kind of trick could it possibly be? How could she help him by encouraging them to kill him? It made no sense. Could she truly mean it?

His legs buckled, and he sank to the ground with his face in the dirt and lay there for he did not know how long. Later, he looked up at the window again; it glowed unreachable as if it hovered a thousand kilometers above him. He yearned to fling himself into the hut, into Bren's arms. But he could not bring himself to set his eyes on her again. He did not know how to make himself hear the sort of thing she might be saying. He slunk away, back to his hiding place.

~•~

"When the Samas took over," Elek went on, "my mother understandably joined with them." He stopped, hearing in his voice that calm rationality with which Jenchae told his own sad tales. He was almost grateful for the catch into his voice when he added, "Unfortunately, that meant she. . ." he had no idea how to put it ". . . she couldn't stand with me."

"What do you mean?" asked Meravyn, incorrigible.

He could not explain what Bren had said. He could not lay that before them and ask them what they thought it meant. Had she abandoned him? Had she not? It wasn't their place to tell him that. If anyone should know, he should. And two hundred years later, he still did not.

He would keep to the facts. Even that was more than he owed them. "She left," he said.

Meravyn thankfully confined her response to staring at him with her galling, big-eyed pity.

At length, Jenchae prodded, "Left?"

"Yes," said Elek, suddenly tired. "And don't ask me for details. I don't know any. We — got separated. I wasn't there when she left."

Jenchae studied the floor.

Why am I telling them this? Elek would rather give it over, be the leaf upon the stream. Lie down in the corner and let the peace seep through him.

Silence stretched across the cell. Elek hoped this would be the end of the their questions but knew it was not.

Finally, predictable as an isotope's decay, Jenchae asked, "What happened to you?"

"I ran. I was caught."

~ • ~

Bad planning. He hadn't even looked for supplies. So he baked all day underneath his rocks as Sama thrust-gliders settled in and soared out. When it was dark, he stumbled out gnawed by thirst and hunger and found a cactus patch that would give at least some nourishment at the cost of bloody fingers.

He would have to get water and over-clothes at least. The easiest place he could think of to break into would be his mother's hut, so he trudged back again. No sound nor light in the room this time.

He crept to the door. But they spotted him as he was reaching for the latch. The rest was a blur.

Shouting in Dab. Figures darted towards him, and he struck out, sending some flying while others seized him and tore at him. He found himself yelling at them desperately: he wasn't a Tral; he was one of them, half-Sama, a slave here; look, he could speak Dab like any native; his mother was a slave here; her name was Bren; they'd talked to her.

At least, he thought he said those things. There was no memory of sound or words, only the fire as the nerve gun hit him and his limbs flung out in all directions.

He awoke secured to a wall with short white ropes around his wrists and ankles. The room looked metallic and completely enclosed: no window, no hint of desert air, like one of the water reclamation rooms built deep into the mountain. But he had never seen this room before. It was small and bright and half filled with black containers. A storage room?

He was alone. He tried to break the ropes, expecting at first that it would be easy. But they did not so much as stretch: some weird synthetic material.

He was extremely thirsty and a little too cold. Would they leave him here to die? Surely, they'd have shot him first. Maybe Bren was negotiating for him now.

Maybe. . .

Time stretched on. At first, he watched the door, dreading it would open, then longing for it to open. His head began to pound with each breath of the unnatural, chemically

air. Finally, he stopped smelling it, but his head kept pounding.
He wondered how long it would take him to die of thirst. He
wondered if Bren would come for him. For a time, he even half-
expected to see her come through the door and set him free. She
did not. Tears stung his eyes and dried. His muscles ached at
their confinement till the ache became a stabbing pain and died
again to an ache. He waited.

He had ceased to watch the door when it whirred open.
He tensed for an attack, ready to struggle as much as his bonds
would let him. A Sama man came in, bringing water. Elek took
the cup awkwardly in his tied hands and gulped the water.

Then he looked at the man. It looked like the one Bren
had spoken to. The man told him they weren't going to hurt
him because it wasn't his fault he was half-Tral. But they
couldn't let him go either because Trals were strong and violent
and couldn't be let free among human people. Elek, he said, had
proven that by putting four of their people in sick-care. So
they'd keep him here till they decided what to do. Maybe they'd
take him to the South where there were more hybrids like
himself.

"Where's Bren?" asked Elek, for the man had to know
she was his mother.

"Gone — to a new town and a new life. Once a slave
here, who'd not choose to go hence?"

Gone? She wouldn't have gone, not without him. Unless
they forced her. Unless they told her he was dead. Unless
they'd tricked her. Unless she was tricking them. Unless she
really did wish to dust her life of him.

"Gone whither?" Perhaps he could find her — if she
wanted to be found.

"I know not," said the man, lying probably. "'Tis no
concern of mine, or thine. She's well enough rid of thee."

Elek did not ask anything more. He knew the futility of
questions. The man took the water cup and went away.

Elek tried to decide which was worse: that room or life in
Shinegray? The room, he thought. It made his eyes throb from
too much light. And at least Shinegray had had its pleasant
moments, its free moments with Apashar and Bren —

He cut the thought off. He was getting good at that.

Sometimes people came to see him, to give him bare necessities and clean a little bit. Different people came at first, most silent and sullen. Some spit at him and kicked him. Someone cursed him for breaking the ribs of someone or other he'd never heard of and slammed a heel into his ribs in recompense. After a while, only one came, a blonde girl who spoke nicely to him of how the town was being rebuilt on the outside. Elek, she explained, was being held in a storeroom on a glider.

Suspecting that the Sama man had lied, Elek asked her if Bren was still in Shinegray. The girl said, "No." She knew everyone in Shinegray, and there was no Bren.

His new companion's name was Colmuan: a real Sama name, like his mother's. . . not at all like the Keshnul names the Trals had given the slaves born under them. Colmuan talked to him as if he were a normal person. She had a bright smile and sky blue eyes that glowed in a tanned face. Her hair, which she tucked behind big ears, was the pale gold of maize tassels. She came like a moonbeam from the living world. After a time, they shared stories and songs, just as friends do.

One day, he told her he would die if he had to stay in that room. The white lights pounded behind his eyes, and the too-chilly recycled air made his head ache with its synthetic smells, and the floor was hard — and he'd die if he couldn't get out into the real world and see the stars and smell the sand on the wind.

Her eyes squeezed up with tears, and she promised that, of course, she would help him escape.

It wasn't really hard, except that Elek was weak from sitting in the room. After all, no one suspected that a Sama would help him, and he couldn't have gotten away on his own. She brought him supplies in a pack and a "molecular code strip," she called it, that she'd filched from her aunt to loosen the ropes. Then, at night, when few guards were awake, she helped him sneak out of the bright-lit ship into the warm starry air that seemed an impenetrable wall of black — for a minute. And then it faded into focus: the West-Hillside as he'd long known it, strange new house-lights glinting over the familiar peaks.

She asked if he knew where he ought to go.

Down the watershed, he told her, where there were
plants to eat and an occasional well. He'd be happy on his own,
he told her. But when she kissed him goodbye, he longed to ask
her to join him, though he knew it was impossible.

Still, they were happy days, those five days he slept out
the sun in shallow caves and drank water in the twilight from
the two old wells each covered over with a boulder, wells the
Trals had dug before the Samas had come with machines to drill
out the deep ground water. He was proud that with his Tral
strength, he could move the boulders. Cactus did not make
good food, but it was enough for now, hunger a small enough
price for freedom.

His days were marred only by the fear that pierced him
when Sama searchers came and he hid, prepared to strike them
dead if they found him. They did not.

On the fifth day at dusk, he heard footsteps nearing and,
heart drumming, dove behind one of the craggy outcroppings
he'd identified as a fair hiding place. Peering into the russet
distance, he could make out the form of Colmuan, stopping here
and there and looking round, doubtless trying to spot him.

He took a breath that staid his heart and rose to meet her.
They did not speak till they were close enough to talk to each
other in whispers.

"'Tis unsafe for thee here," he told her.

"And for thee." Her mouth was drawn into a frown that
threatened to break into weeping any moment.

"Thou looks wretched," he said.

"They'll not leave thee be here. They behold in thee a
wild creature to be contained, even for the safety of the children.
They'll kill thee." She paused. "Unless thou come with us now."

Elek stiffened. "Us?" he echoed, "Whom has thou
betrayed me to?"

She shifted her feet. "My aunt, she guessed that I had
taken her key to free thee. She had the truth of me, Elek" — now
she stared up at him earnestly — "only because I would not see
thee slain. She and my uncle will take thee to safety in the
South; she has sworn it."

Elek felt very quiet inside, like a small, heavy stone
incapable of motion. "They are here now?"

"Yea, waiting."

She would have them take him back. Colmuan, whom
he had trusted, would have him placed again the prisons of her
people. Imprisoned or shot. They would not take him to the
South. Why should they? And she knew it; she must know. She
was simply standing with them. Her people. She was merely
one of them. A coward. A soft, weak fool, there trembling
before him like an insect grub.

A flame ignited him. He seized her by the neck and
flung her as far as he could. She crashed into a rock with a dull
thump and collapsed like a rag doll, coughing blood
disgustingly. There came a shriek from above and the zing of a
nerve gun.

In terror, Elek fled.

~•~

"The Samas held me prisoner for a while: I'd guess not
more than half a month. It felt like more."

Elek wanted to turn from the pity in their eyes. Why was
he telling them this? Because Jenchae had been demanding to
know since their first day together. Because Meravyn, too, had a
brutal need for understanding.

There was no understanding. He could pull every detail
from his darkest memory and lay it out bright white before
them, and still they would never understand.

"Finally, a girl helped me escape. I hid in a nearby valley
for a few days, until they tried to recapture me. They found me.
They tried to shoot me, so I just ran." All night, in the light of
the moons he had run, stopping only when his legs collapsed
beneath him, resting only long enough to make them work
again. Long, long after the voices had faded.

"By morning I had made it almost down to the
flatlands." He stopped. "Well, not really. I was still in the
Foots. But it was the nearest to flat land I'd ever seen. When I'd
gathered my wits, I remembered the old rule that you follow
down the watershed, so I headed for the low land down a ravine
and came to a spot where some marula trees were growing. I
slept there. When I woke up, I remember eating the marula fruit
and getting drunk and sick. That night, when I was a little
better, I kept following the 'shed down, till I found a well. I

stayed there for maybe a month, pretty malnourished, I suppose. I watched the thrust-gliders coming and going."

He could picture them now, sleek as long-winged, white birds swooping over the hills with an airy roar. He remembered thinking they could have been the insignia of freedom.

He looked at the floor tiles to avoid their eyes. "From the flight pattern of the gliders, I gathered that there was another town several kilometers west of me. Finally, I decided to head for it, thinking maybe I could stow away on one of the gliders and get to the South-lands. To keep it short, that's what I did."

~ • ~

Should he go on?

Should he tell them how for days after he had killed Colmuan, he'd been sick to his stomach at the thought of her? How he had hated himself more than he had ever dreamed possible? How in his dreams, she got all mixed up with his mother, and he, a small, unknowing child once again, would get angry and push her like children do, and she'd fall and be dead, this Bren-Colmuan. And staring with frosted eyes, she'd say, "You know you made me leave. How could anyone stay with you?"

In his waking hours, he had tried to make sense of it. It was a mistake. He had been surprised. It was a betrayal, something she had deserved. Deserved? Mistake? Best to put it all behind him. Start over and do better. In the days he had waited to sneak aboard the glider, he had vowed he would never kill again.

But in the city, there was no work, no way to live but thieving. And thieves met violence. And he was good at violence. Then one day, that corpse collector had seen him fight and hired him. He'd told himself it was just for the money, just eliminating people who must have done something very wrong for other people to want them dead. It was work. That was all.

But he didn't believe it. And the self-hate came back, fiercer month by month. Should he explain to them that he'd quit the work because he didn't want to be one of *those* people? The killers. Explain how hard he'd tried to do normal work at normal jobs? Explain how willingly he'd gone into therapy when his temper got him fired? Again. And again.

And then, he'd gone to work in the marula groves. He had been happy there — Meravyn knew. He had come to believe that this time it wouldn't matter if he couldn't pay for his mood suppressants. He had discovered his place; he didn't need the drugs. He'd stopped taking them, and everything had been all right — until that day when suddenly it wasn't. And there lay his friend, dead at his feet, and when he wondered where all that peace had gone, it occurred to him that it had come from —

The drugs.

Peace. Like floating down a stream, like resting in the rain. Like lying suspended light years away from all the things that ought to make the outraged blood sizzle.

Jenchae had done it to him again.

As Elek looked into that patient face, his limbs even now resisted motion with an unnatural, numbing fatigue. "What did you do?" he asked low.

Jenchae didn't need to read his mind to grasp the accusation. Elek could see him square his jaw. "I gave you a suggestion of quiet to quench the rage."

"Gouging my mind one more time." Elek laughed. "I don't know how in hell you managed it — but you did. I'm not even angry at you *now*. Not like I ought to be. Just tranqued all over again."

"Jenchae?" Meravyn's sharp voice, wary.

"It was a suggestion," Jenchae repeated, his face immobile. "But it's in your own mind; I'm not enforcing it."

"Then why can't I shake this?" Elek asked. "Why can't I find my rage at you?"

"If you truly want to," said Jenchae, "if you want to feel a need to kill me —"

"Getting to it."

" — then you can. It's just a crutch. Throw it down." He paused. "You once told me you wanted sedation. Remember? Sedation without me in your mind. Well, you have it." Jenchae turned away, then sighed. "But it isn't what you really wanted. Or not what you want anymore. It was wrong of me. Wrong again. I'm sorry."

Cheap words, Jenchae. Going around in the same circle. Again and —

A silent understanding dawned in Elek's thoughts. "Oh, Jenchae. You are falling into a pit, my friend."

Jenchae raised his hands in a helpless gesture. "There's no time for you to learn Mind-taxing; that's the work of months, years. I don't know how else to help you."

"Forget *me* for a minute. Take a look at yourself. You think it's getting better, what you do to me. You think you've been tampering less. After all, first you took hold of my body, and then you just sat in my mind, and now you're trying — what? — mere 'suggestions.' No. You're losing yourself. That first time, you attacked me by instinct — self-preservation; I still don't understand why it bothered you so much. Later, yes, you came in at my invitation — but you didn't want to let go, did you? Not even when I begged you. Now, you're on to meddling without my knowledge or consent, as if I were your plaything. Where do you go next?"

They all sat in silence, Jenchae's face contorted as he frowned at the floor. Finally, he whispered, "Then, there's no way I can help you."

Elek laughed again, this time with a comfortingly comprehensible prickle of agitation. "It's taken you an awfully long time to discover what I told you the day we met. *Now* you see: you can't help me. Thank you, Jenchae. Thank you for absolutely nothing." He turned away and did his best not to feel anything: not rage, not peace, not rest. Nothing.

CHAPTER SEVENTEEN

To live in the fear of death is not life. True life
swoops like a swallow, fearless, faster than the
eye can follow.

Leng Ázoram, Address on the Eve of the Last
Stand on Zeinnéfa* (1299 B.E.)

"I'm going to the lav," said Meravyn.
She needed to be alone, to sit in the corner of the little,
faintly foul-smelling space, her foot against the base of the toilet.
There was a comforting solidity in an object to rest a foot on: not
like the slick cell outside.
When had a cell become "outside"?
She was trying not to despise Jenchae. She understood
he'd wanted to keep them safe, to give Elek some solace. But
Elek had been right. Jenchae had lost his consci— his judgment.

---

* Compare: "Death is soil to the roots of life," from *The Wisdom of
Letting Die* by Samlla of the Fallingwind House (781 B.E.)

Author's Note

Zeinnéfa is the original name of the planet R'Aej, which was
ceded by the Ranlans to the ancestors of the Ash'torians after the
planet's Ranlan population was defeated in a military coup.
Ázoram led the Ranlan counter-resistance movement and was
killed. For his heroism, he was posthumously named Clan-
Founder Abte'nyq.

Translator's Note

How else could he justify such deception, manipulation, especially when life had already battered Elek so fiercely. . .

Imagine being caught by the Samas of Tenstar.

She was ashamed that, like Jenchae, she'd urged Elek to speak of his life. Morbidly, she had longed to see what had made him who he was.

Now, she felt dirty that she'd let herself listen. She had made him a spectacle, an exotic caged creature to gawk at. He hadn't wanted to share those things.

Her eyes came to rest on a corner of the toilet's base, two planes meeting, a right angle defined by orange reflecting on black. It gave the impression of a distortion in space: time bending. Or being bent. Souls being bent. People trapped in a cell together, in a mind together, twisting each other.

Was this the plan of Ash'tor?

Even if it was, that did not absolve her. She had let him lay his life before her and had found it diverting.

~ • ~

Elek watched Jenchae sit eyes closed by the wall.

We can give thanks for that anyway. Elek didn't want to deal with the man.

He should be angry at Jenchae, but the damn suggestion dulled everything. Even now, he longed to let the stream bear him away. If anything, he was perturbed with himself. He shouldn't have talked of those days. Bren and Colmuan and — he ought to be outraged, guilty, disgusted. But he wasn't. His heart beat evenly; his breathing came slow; his hands were cool despite the cell's slight mugginess. And though he fought to stay alert, he rested far away, as if watching himself through a frosted glass.

Could Jenchae truly have wanted this numbness for him? The calm, yes, — but the numbness? Was this blankness Jenchae's doing at all — or was this just Elek's way of defending himself now that Jenchae's myth of peace had been stripped?

All this temperance was too much like before. Before this cell, before Jenchae. Mild moments when it seemed nothing could touch him, when the rage had a soft unreality. But it was a lie. The rage always returned.

Yet it had to be different now, didn't it? Because this calm he could keep hold of even while speaking of those things, things which for decades he hadn't let himself remember.

Maybe that was the way Jenchae had programmed him.

Or could it be he had finally learned the things Jenchae had promised?

In any case, calm was a good thing, wasn't it?

So why was he sure he was still doing wrong?

~•~

Jenchae's back ached. He got up, shuffled to the cot, lay down. As he settled in, he scraped his shoulder on the top edge of the cot alcove, so his shoulder hurt too. *Little pains build up like life.*

His contempt for himself was rearing to tidal proportions. *Don't think about it. Self-contempt is just another form of wallowing.*

Elek's tale had explained the rage. It didn't matter that Elek had given them only a sketch of his life. By Jenchae's age, you could paint in the rest. *I'd already known nine-tenths of that story — of the feel of it — just from feeling it in his mind.* Yes, it explained Elek.

What it didn't explain to Jenchae was Jenchae.

All the time we've been here, I've been pushing him to talk about himself. I told myself that if he did, I could help him. What in hell was I thinking? Was I trying to help at all? Am I just the voyeur he accused me of being? Am I worse? Am I Akhté, a tyrant of minds? Have I ever truly desired to help my society — or all my life, have I merely sought control?

I have controlled him — but I can't help him. I can't even speak to him. What am I supposed to say? "I'm sorry"? "I'm sorry I've toyed with your mind and gave you nothing. I'm sorry you're one more victim of a defective society"? Like me, like Akhté, except for you, it was worse.

But I've heard stories worse than all of ours. There are people who have suffered worse, turned out worse. People who have suffered worse and turned out better.

Doesn't matter. It's not a contest.

And there's nothing I can do about it. There never was.

~•~

It puts things in perspective, Meravyn thought. *I thought Trenod had troubles. And he did. But compared to Elek, he always fared well. Stable parents. Stable home.*

He never needed me.

Certainly, in some ways I was good for him. We had merry times.

But never need.

If I'd never come to the Ybian Homeworld to save him, what would have happened? They'd have taken him prisoner, back to Manyrock — or maybe to one of the Trae'dah worlds. He would have been unhappy, but he would have been alive and well-known enough to make demands for himself. They'd not have executed him. They'd not even have tried him for deserting the Nation.

All those years wracked with worry for him. . . Years, too, of indignation at Ash'tor. In all those years, I never truly had to fight, never had to kill. I couldn't imagine the kind of living these men here have seen.

It grants perspective as a gift, Elek's story. The aloneness of it.

Yet like all beings, finally, he needs belonging. To be part of the family of peoples. He needs that from me. I'm here, and he needs me. Trenod never did, but he does.

~ • ~

Elek sighed. With Jenchae, of course, it had been a debacle, but at least he could blame Jenchae for that — or for much of it. The weight he couldn't shift was Meravyn.

She was still hiding in the lav, and he understood why. For a moment, early on, it seemed he'd won her camaraderie, if only by virtue of being another Tral. They had spoken in their own tongue of vanished, dreamlike things, of trees and sand and seasons.

And then he had told her about Ned'yem. Naturally, after that, she would shun him. It didn't matter that he hadn't said he'd killed Colmuan. Probably she could guess. Probably she was terrified. And sympathetic too. Kind to him because she pitied him — enough to keep talking to him, to sit next to him. And all the things he'd said just now doubtless made her feel sorrier for him. Sorrier but determined to keep away.

Because he wasn't normal. The stagnancy inside him right now proclaimed that. But it was worse than just "abnormal": bit by bit he'd shown her a divide between them as uncrossable as the Lus on foot. They were just a few meters away from each other but as far apart as South from North.

She was a child of the South, of the Truce: of ordinary family and schools and jobs. And no normal person would be fool enough to entangle herself with him.

~ • ~

When there is nothing left to do, there's peace.

No. Jenchae would have laughed at himself if he'd had the energy. This wasn't peace. In this room, there wasn't an oxygen molecule he sucked into his lungs that had peace.

But when there's nothing left to do, there are no mistakes. No more responsibility.

Jenchae exhaled, the load lightened. He'd made himself responsible for so many lives for so long, he didn't know how to live any other way. He'd been a leader, a helper. Tamperer, dominator. Living without that responsibility was the first lesson perhaps. Or the last. It didn't matter. *When there's no future, only the moment matters.* And for the moment, he was tired.

~ • ~

When Meravyn stepped out of the lav, some great resolution slipped away from her. She stood there, looking around. Jenchae was on his back on the cot, his useless hands lax at his sides. She scarcely had to glance at him to know he was asleep. That was how often she'd seen him sleeping.

Elek was sitting at the far wall, watching her.

She took a step toward him and stopped. Weird how his eyes tracked her movement — like a primitive interactive robot. For a moment, she was sure she would have to run, even if right into a wall.

Perhaps she should say something: *"I'm glad you told us,"* or *"I'm sorry we made you tell us,"* or *"Everything will be all right"* — because *that* was believable.

There were no words.

She sat down by his side, his eyes on her all the while. After several seconds, she turned toward him, put her fingers to his cheek. It was awkward, uncomfortable, entirely the wrong gesture. He raised his hand to hers and pulled it down in his own hands, a little cooler than hers — and suddenly it all felt less strange.

"I'm sorry, Meravyn."

That startled her. "For what?"

He said nothing for a while, eyes on her hand, rubbing it slowly with his fingers. "Everything."

Something in his sad tone made her stronger. All hesitation gone, she caught him in a close hug. For a second, he tensed, then returned her embrace, arms firm around her back.

The last time she'd known such simple closeness had been before she'd left Manyrock, when her sister had hugged her that last day.

"Thou and I," she said to Elek, "will walk the last lap together." But those words were inadequate.

When she drew back, he refused to meet her eyes. He did not understand. How could she tell him he was not alone? People touched minds to say so, but that could not help him.

Meravyn sighed and leaned her head against the wall, feeling compassion for Jenchae. He had wanted to ease Elek's pain, to show himself his life meant something because he could ease it — and so did she. And neither of them could. All at once her chest contracted.

"Meravyn, why are you here?" Elek asked.

She glanced at Elek, startled. He knew why: the explosion, the five dead. . . Or was he baiting her about Trenod?

"You mean to tell me I'm here because I loved him too much?" she challenged.

His face froze. He shook his head and turned away again. She'd said the wrong thing; he'd misunderstood. There had to be another way, had to be words to say how she'd discovered her life here with him.

~ • ~

Back to Trenod! Elek's body clenched. He looked straight ahead, afraid of what he would do if he moved. Nothing in her mind but that man. Yet she could put her arms around Elek and speak of going to death with him — incomprehensible, her befriending him. Why reach out to Elek? Why him?

It was vital he know, but when asked, all her thoughts were of Trenod. Again.

A furnace sweltered in his chest. He could picture metal melting and the fire spewing out and —

It hit him that she had broken through.

She'd overpowered Jenchae's suggestion; he was himself again. So great was Elek's relief for a second that the anger sputtered. He could have kissed her.

But he couldn't kiss her because she belonged to that other. She wore it like a martyr's noose, her self-enslavement.

Meravyn drew a breath, the kind someone draws when trying to be patient with an exasperating child — as if Elek were merely tiresome now. "You know," she said (Elek couldn't tell if she meant him or Jenchae) "among every people, there's a question: how much do you live for yourself, and how much for others? Take the Ash'torians: they live for others. . ."

She paused as if she were expecting an objection, but Elek did not trust himself to speak, and Jenchae just lay there, gazing at her.

She went on, "We don't see it that way, of course. We see them using us for their own benefit, but I'm talking about individuals, not whole societies. Ash'torians define themselves in terms of family and colleagues and their responsibilities to them." Again she paused.

What does this have to do with anything? wondered Elek.

"Would you agree with that, Jenchae?" Meravyn asked.

"Yes, why not?" He sounded as if he were agreeing to tag along on someone else's outing.

"All right. Well, Manyrock is more oriented around 'self-definition,' I'll call it. We have bonds to our loved ones, but we emphasize individual accomplishment. My sister takes pride in being known throughout the South as an irrigation specialist. Now, my sister never approved of my marriage. She warned me that Trenod was going to be trouble because his hypertelepathy caused him all those difficulties."

Trenod's difficulties! Elek strove not to hiss between his teeth.

"She said I threw my life away on him," Meravyn insisted on continuing. "And Elek, you told me much the same."

"Evidence you should listen maybe," he retorted without meaning to have spoken.

Meravyn snapped her eyes onto him, tense, motionless. In the silence, he longed to twist her head away. "It's difficult," she said at last. "In a way, you're right. Here I am —" she cast a glance at the cell "— about to die — for him. But if I choose to define myself through another, isn't that still my choice? My self-definition?"

We've been through this before, haven't we? Or was that Ned'yem? She used to go on like this. Heaping up words.

"Is that a question?" asked Jenchae after a moment.

"No," said Meravyn.

Jenchae smiled marginally.

"It is my choice," said Meravyn, "as surely as the choice to become an irrigation specialist or a botanist."

That comparison vexed Elek. Meravyn had studied botany. It was a field Elek would have studied if he'd gone to school. But she was saying that wasn't the path she'd chosen — she'd chosen Trenod. And she was far too sanctimoniously proud of it.

It ran deeper than that, though. *Choice.* The concept was so ludicrous he'd have laughed at her if he wasn't so annoyed. Oh surely, there were choices of a sort in this life: go here or go there; shoot or don't shoot. But what did all that mean when it came down to it? What made "there" better than "here" when you'd rather be neither place? And what kind of choice was kill-or-be-killed when you just want to be left alone?

"It's all a question of what you choose to do with yourself," Meravyn persisted.

If she tells me I've done the wrong things with myself — If she thinks I need her to tell me —

She was watching him too closely. "I've been told I've been wrong to define myself so much by Trenod. But there is nothing wrong with finding yourself in others. A person, any person, is beyond description. To know one person is the art of a lifetime. There could not be better work."

Elek cackled. He had had enough. "Your capacity for self-delusion, Meravyn, is 'beyond description,' at any rate. Both of you," he glanced at Jenchae, who looked back warily.

"You're not listening," said Meravyn. "My point is —"

"I know what your point is. You're after meaning and choice and *knowing* people. And you think you can have those things, but you can't. You think you can get me to believe in these paradise pictures you've painted in your head. But you can't because *I* — I know they're not real." Poor Meravyn! Her face was so grave, like a child who'd mistaken a joke for reality. No — rather one who'd mistaken reality for a bad joke and kept on waiting for the joke to be over, not realizing that there was nothing else.

"What's real is this," he told her: "every life is pain; every life is death. And pain and death are what we're left with in the long run. The Sama Empire fell, and the remnants of the Samas fought the Trals; then the Ash'torians conquered them both. So goes life. Everything we call 'good' is netted up in suffering or killing — or both: food, feeling, birth, sex, seeing, hearing. . . civilization, love, peace. Nothing —" he groped for a way to say it " — nothing excises the hurting from it. No, not even talking about it, Jenchae."

"But I'm glad that you talked to us, Elek," said Meravyn, "About yourself, I mean. Even if didn't ease your pain, at least it taught me something."

"Oh, you think so?" Elek almost laughed. "There's nothing in it, Meravyn. Nothing. You think you'll have insight into me if I explain how I felt when my mother said I'd be better off dead? I could spend years telling you everything I know about my life, and nothing that I say would be anything but banal. Experiences shared by billions. In billions of ways. For eons." He paused, picturing of eons of lives stretching across light centuries like galaxies built of raw neurons. "It's the sand that makes the desert. It's the universe."

It felt good to say. It made him feel like the universe and he were one. . . .

When had he come to think that?

Meravyn was fixing him with a measuring, cold stare.

Slowly, she said, "What you told us made me to cast new eyes back on Trenod."

Now that is just insulting.

"I've heard enough about Trenod."

"You are still missing my point," she said, taking his hand — he almost pulled away but didn't. "I looked back and found myself again in you."

So *that* was what he was to her. Her latest effort at "self-definition." She might as well have told him that he was a botanical survey, her latest project. "I'm not a mirror for you to look into, Meravyn. I'm not clay for you to mold. I'm not your work."

Her hand tightened on his. "I'm not talking about molding you. Mad gods, do you think I tried to make *him* over in my image?" Her voice cut like a saw.

"And I am most certainly not your substitute Trenod." He got to his feet, inadvertently pulling her up with him.

"I'd never expect you to be," she said, still gripping his hand. "I've only known you a few days; I knew him most of my life."

And I'll never be what he was to you. I know.

Her condescension sickened him, almost as much as her palm sweating against his.

Fluidly, he snaked his free hand around, seized her neck, slammed her back hard against the wall in a burst of satisfaction. She was squirming, eyes disoriented. Mesmerized by her writhing, he moved in close.

Dimly, he could hear Jenchae shout, a cry lost in thunder.

Then she lunged against him, and pain stabbed his ribs. He stumbled back, gasping.

He'd pulled in too close —

An amateur's mistake —

Her elbow —

The thoughts had scarcely formed when she punched him in the face. He staggered, exhilarated. It had been a long time since a Tral had fought him back.

He recovered himself, spinning round to face her, years of battle experience clicking. Her face, red, distorted with fury, looked farther away than he knew it was. Jenchae, a blur in his peripheral vision, was bobbing up and down, still yelling, inconsequential.

He sprang at Meravyn. She aimed another blow — obvious. He deflected it with his left hand and, with his right, seized her neck again and smashed her to the ground. Jenchae was there somewhere. With his free hand, Elek batted him away. Meravyn was trying gamely to kick him. Let her try — she wouldn't win.

~ • ~

When Jenchae saw it coming, he scrambled up from the cot, distantly aware that his scrabbling burned his hands. Didn't matter. His eyes were on Meravyn. She kept trying to explain and couldn't see that he couldn't listen.

"Stop," he commanded. "Step back, both of you."

But the words came too late, and Elek's hand was around her thoat. Her head struck the wall with a crack of a percussion gun. Too late. She was —

No, she was a Tral. She was alive, still moving, feeling: confusion, panic, fury.

And Elek burned in circles in the fires of his brain. If Jenchae was going to save her — to save both of them, he must act. Now. He must take Elek's mind —

Then she kicked out. She was free. Jenchae shook with relief. No, he didn't need to. She could take care of herself. He hugged the wall, well clear of their stony bodies.

But now, Elek had her down again, and she was struggling, but he was stronger and —

Jenchae shouted; he didn't know what. No one heard him.

Must make him pull back.

But he couldn't, not that way. Not again. Not that again. It wasn't — It wouldn't solve —

But he had to act.

Desperately, he stumbled forward, wrapping his arms around Elek's waist. Hands exploding in white-hot flame, he tugged with all his might. He screamed, "You must stop! You can stop!" His foot tripped against Meravyn's flailing leg. He fell against Elek, and Elek swiped him, like a cat with broken-winged bird, one fluid movement and Jenchae was sprawled by the wall, vision swimming, scarcely able to pull air into his lungs.

~ • ~

177

Yes — Elek almost smiled — this was a fight he would
win.

Win?

In a moment, she'd be dead.

The thought iced through his chest.

Yes — because he hated her thoroughly now, hated. . .

Himself. Not her.

Himself. . . for this.

In a sudden self-revulsion, he let go of her and turned
away. As he turned, he saw Jenchae crumpled by the wall,
gasping, holding his hands up like helpless mouse paws — the
hands Elek had broken.

In a second, he was at Jenchae's side, holding him up,
though Jenchae shrank away. Elek helped him lean into the
corner, then let go and took a step back.

Meravyn was struggling up, coughing.

It had all come out wrong again, as he knew it would.

At the center of the room, he stopped. The echo of the
smack of her head on the floor seemed to follow him instant by
instant.

Wrong — like everything.

I'm everyone. Their wrongs are mine.

He made himself breathe and turn to face them.
Meravyn stood clutching the back of her neck and glowering like
a Tral from Shinegray: hard and white and insurmountable, and
he a rodent cornered. There was a sweet excitement in it.

He glanced to Jenchae, still wheezing in the corner, his
face taut, his mind a wall.

"Finish it!" Meravyn croaked. "Finish me now; you think
that means you'll defeat me?"

Perhaps he shook his head. After a moment, he laughed
raggedly.

"You're insane!" she cried out and backed up a step. A
minute or more clipped past in time with her breathing. At last,
calmer, Meravyn said, "Unplug your ears. I do not want you to
be Trenod or my work or anything of mine. I had thought my
life was over. You made me see I am still alive — as long as I
can act for another's life. And I chose yours. Not because you're
lesser or greater or better or worse than Trenod. Not anything to

do with him. Because I saw you. You." She pointed a finger at him accusingly. "And it is not <u>nothing</u>!"

Elek was trying to listen to her, but her words, like water skimmers, kept floating over the surface.

"Then what am I?" he asked.

She stood very still. "A person I've shared life with."

Not about Trenod? She had been reaching out to Elek. Imperfectly, selfishly perhaps — but to him.

He sank to the floor, suddenly aware of his burning ribs and aching jaw. And Meravyn's throat was turning purple.

"Meravyn. How you must hate me."

She sank down opposite him, her back against the wall. "I do *not* hate." Her eyes were still smoldering.

He'd tried to kill her, and she didn't hate him. Didn't hate.

"Jenchae?" He turned to Jenchae, still staring at them from his corner.

Jenchae shook his head dumbly. "All right. I'm all right," he whispered.

No malice behind those words; Jenchae, too, had never hated him. That simple fact: *I tried to kill him too. All I've done to him! And he never hated me.* How had that miracle never struck him before? It was. . . beyond description, Meravyn had said. *People are beyond description.*

"You let her go." Jenchae's voice, soft.

"I almost killed her."

"But you didn't."

"Only because I'm a Tral," said Meravyn. "If I were weak as a human, I'd be dead."

"I know," said Jenchae softly. "Yet he did let you go."

It was true, Elek reflected. Never before had he let anyone leave the grips of rage alive. He'd been forced away, fought off by some, but never *let* anyone go.

"You've done me good, both of you," he whispered.

"I should think so," Meravyn snapped. "You have no right to be angry at me. I owe you nothing."

No, she didn't, did she?

"I'm not angry at you," he told her truthfully.

"I owe no one," she said quieter, as if to herself, massaging the back of her head where it had struck the floor. Where he had struck her. . .

But then — he'd let her go.

"Jenchae," said Elek, "am I learning?"

Jenchae hesitated. "You must be."

Meravyn scoffed. "Learning," she muttered under her breath.

"You —" he wasn't sure which one he meant. "You've given me —"

Meravyn turned her face away. That cut him. He wished he could make her understand what he meant, like she had tried to make him understand. Understanding was impossible. But maybe that didn't matter. They were here all the same.

Elek lay back on the floor and looked up at the dull circles glowing on the ceiling and felt Meravyn and Jenchae all around. It came as a kind of warmth, like a candle in the dark, like a tiny star pinpricks the blackness of space.

CHAPTER EIGHTEEN

The riddle of Sham'taht cannot be uttered. The
soul prepared to comprehend it will breathe it in
as easily as air.

Tales of the Nine Clans (c. 800 B.E.)

Sometimes the gods walk your way. Jenchae's mother used
to say that on the occasions when chance did them a favor. He
said it to himself now, despite throbbing hands and aching head
and ribs that stung when he breathed. He'd breathe easier lying
down, no doubt. But he'd rather be up and active.

So he sat by the cot, Meravyn by the adjacent wall,
massaging her neck. Elek was on his back on the floor, his feet
crossed, looking comfortable.

Jenchae had been watching Elek a long time. An almost-
smile came and went across his face. Elek had reason to be glad.
He had stopped himself from killing Meravyn. He had done it
himself. He'd done it. He'd succeeded. And so had Jenchae.

When Elek had attacked Meravyn, Jenchae's first instinct
had been to hurl him back, to clamp down on his brain and
make him let her go. It would have been easy after all the time
their minds had touched, almost as easy as thinking his own
thoughts. Yet he had refrained. And, in the end, Elek had
refrained as well. So perhaps Jenchae had helped him after all.
And perhaps Elek had helped Jenchae too.

Now, Jenchae was wide awake, watching the shiftings
and poppings of his world.

He was subdued too, nagged by the awareness that this
happy outcome was partly luck. What if Elek hadn't let
Meravyn go? What if Meravyn couldn't fight him off? She'd be

dead because Jenchae had not helped her. And how would he feel about himself then?

That was a question he could not answer and was well advised not to dwell on.

Elek had learned. And Jenchae had done his part; now, he could disappear.

There was a flicker and blackness. For an instant, it struck Jenchae that some god — walking his way! — had overheard him. *And now I have disappeared indeed.*

Then came Elek's voice from the center of the room: "Nice job they did on that fault with the lights."

Silence a moment. "'They' or autorepair." Meravyn, still by the wall. "Or maybe they're toying with us — but I don't think so. Not after that attack. I think — I think autorepair is breaking down. Maybe 'they' are long gone." A pause. "It's been a long time since our food's come."

She was right. Jenchae hadn't realized it till now, but the hunger had been creeping on him. He found himself longing for that bland, white rice. Or anything white. Light. He pushed down the fear. He was thirsty too but —

"We should be able to get water from the lav sink," he said. "It should be a simple mechanism — the last thing to stop working."

An almost-scoff from Meravyn's direction. "That should tell us something when it stops, then."

"I don't see why we should bother," said Elek.

"You're ready to die, really?" said Meravyn, a fractional panic in her voice. "Because that's what's happening. We're going to die here now."

"And thank the gods; it's about time." There was a soft fabric noise; perhaps he'd sat up.

Jenchae began to inch down to the corner and up the wall to Meravyn, putting too much pressure on his hands as he went. When he bumped into her, he said her name so that she wouldn't be startled. She jumped anyway, then threaded her arm through his. He could hear the low hum of her mind beside him. She was getting calmer. He himself was comforted by the solidness of her arm.

So we'll die here — but not alone. Sometimes the gods walk our way.

~ • ~

A realization shocked Meravyn bolt upright. "If the systems are failing, maybe the door lock's off." She let go of Jenchae's arm and crept on hands and knees toward the door. Her head still pounded from Elek's assault, the pain magnified by the awkward upward tilt that her swollen neck strained into as she crawled. Electrical impulses in her optic nerve sent swirls across her field of vision, the only reminder that she wasn't blind. She could hear Elek parallel to her, sliding along toward the door. A desire to repulse him vied with her longing for his help.

After what seemed far too great a distance, her questing fingers brushed the door, brushed Elek's fingers already on it. She drew her hand away from his.

"It opens to the left," she said. "So let's push left."

They heaved at the slick door as best they could. It didn't budge, of course. Even if the lock had failed, the door itself was probably too heavy to shift. And without a handle, most of the force they could exert just pushed back against it, not left.

Still, for an absurd, frustrating time, they tried. She could hear Elek breathing hard by the time they gave up.

"Not so eager to die, Elek?" she asked him, out of breath herself.

"Just tired of being in this cell."

"Well, we won't be here long at this rate anyway," replied Meravyn, wishing that someone would contradict her. No one did. She could hear Elek move off toward Jenchae. She followed him, wanting the reassuring pressure of Jenchae's arm again.

Her groping hand found a shoulder that led down to a hand — a healthy hand that took hers firmly. Elek, not Jenchae. She almost jerked away. He didn't deserve her touch.

He'd made her sore, afraid, debased. Furious.

Uncertain, she was still gripping his hand.

Yet what he'd done to her — those things had been done to him for most of his childhood, perhaps most of his life.

No wonder he had rage. The thought did not dispel her own anger, but it softened the edge, as the sunset softens the summer. She disengaged her hand from his and wrapped her arm through his arm as she had with Jenchae, then settled back against the wall, her shoulder to his.

She listened to Elek and Jenchae breathing. The longer they sat, the more intolerable it seemed that they would sit and sit in the blackness, in the silence till their deaths.

Finally, she burst out, "I never imagined I'd die like this, not even after I was sentenced. This is worse than execution."

"Been executed before, have you?" said Elek.

Meravyn was surprised at how grateful she was for the joke.

"Well, if I have to die like this," said Jenchae, "of hunger or thirst or asphyxiation or cold —"

"Do go on," Elek interrupted.

" — I'm glad I am with the two of you."

"Thank you," said Elek. "It's nice to know you can please your companions with your long, drawn-out demise."

She could hear Jenchae attempt a laugh. Being here was not so horrible when they were talking. It reminded Meravyn that they were still alive.

"Is there anything that we can do?" she asked.

"Sing another song?" said Elek.

"I'm serious."

"Seriously," said Jenchae, "what could we do? You tried the door. We've searched the cell. We could try yelling, I suppose. But if no one has come to help us yet, then either there's no one to hear us, or whoever is out there wants us kept here. What else is there to do?"

What else? What else?

"Well, let's try yelling," said Meravyn. "We don't have anything to lose."

They yelled. Elek laughed as much as he yelled. No one came. Meravyn's throat, already raw, grew tighter and tighter with suppressed sobs. None of it helped. Nothing would help!

They lapsed into silence again.

At some point, Elek's hand pressed Meravyn's forearm. For a moment, she wanted to shrug him off. And then, all at

once, she found the light pressure comforting. It made her want
to talk again, to remind herself they were listening.

"This is crazy," she whispered. "Do you know I'm sore
all the time in this cell from sitting on this hard floor. Life
should never be like this."

"But it is," said Elek. "It just is. It is for everyone. Full of
hard floors."

Meravyn could hear the swish of cloth as Jenchae shifted
his position on the other side of Elek. The sound was concrete, a
sign of existence. But Elek had said everything came to nothing,
as if there were no life at all. Hard floors and no life.

"It isn't nothing, though," she said. "If life is like this for
everyone — in some metaphorical way — then that means
everyone's alike, isn't that so?"

"You've got it," said Elek.

"Enemies are friends and friends are enemies — all
stumbling along together. Gods, I'm scared."

"We're all scared," came Jenchae's quiet voice.

"Of course, we are," said Elek. "The universe is full of
monsters."

"I don't care about the universe," said Meravyn. "I feel
so outside the universe here."

"But you're not outside it. Everyone is living this. Our
enemies, who are also our friends, who are also ourselves. It's a
lot to be afraid of — and nothing really."

Again with the nothing! Meravyn thought in passing, but
Elek's words resonated. *Enemies aren't enemies. They are
ourselves.* There was something there, if only she could
remember, an idea she'd had once. There was a way to explain
it, to wrench the feeling into words. A sort of symbol. A sort of
poem.

It was the plant! Her "monster," she'd called it. She had
tried to explain it to Ata once. Ata hadn't understood, but
maybe Elek and Jenchae could.

~ • ~

Elek was not surprised that it was Meravyn, again, who
broke the silence. But he was surprised to hear her say, "Elek,
you said we should sing a song —"

"I was pretty much kidding."

"Good, because I'm not planning to sing. But I do have a story, one I'd like to tell, you know, before the end." She paused, and the seconds stretched out. "And no, it has nothing to do with *him*."

Elek laughed. "In that case, let's certainly hear it." To think no more than a few hours ago he had been ready to kill her over *him* — and now they could joke.

After some seconds, Meravyn said, "I remember a time — I told you how I worked in soil chemistry, and then I lost my job? Well, later, I got a job in the botanical garden out by Blue Stone Lake. It was another. . . it was an Ash'torian place. But that doesn't matter now, I suppose. They had this wisteria. It was a big, prize-winning one. You know what a wisteria looks like?"

"No," said Jenchae. Elek did.

"It's a sort of viny tree," said Meravyn, "with soft, ovate leaves and flowers in long racemes and, well, they had this one. It was — how to put it? — the pride of anyone who didn't have to look after it, a huge viny thing that would snake out over its scaffolding sooner than you could cut it back. My coworkers and I used to joke that it was our *golef,* a death plant — like in children's horror tales — those ones that tangle people up and suck their blood."

Elek remembered his mother's tales of the *golef.* Yes, he could imagine one as a great wisteria.

"Well, one day it was my day to prune it," Meravyn continued. "People had been avoiding the job, and it had climbed up over the greenhouse ceiling. . . roof, I mean — it wasn't *in* the greenhouse. Some fool had planted it right next to the greenhouse. Its branches had climbed across the pathway between its base and the greenhouse wall, and it was clambering over the roof. So I took the ladder and shears and went at it. I set up the ladder on the walk between the plant and the wall, and I climbed up."

She paused. "A breeze was blowing through the leaves and flowers, like the wind through a giant's hair. I climbed up, and the leaves patted my face like feathers, and the perfume of the flowers, all purple, just cascaded. I put my hand to the tendrils, the baby ones, all inoffensive: no thorns, no stings, no gum gluing my fingers. I cut them and dropped them to the ground. And there they lay, without complaint. I felt so guilty — I remember thinking to the bush that it only meant that it would need less water to feed fewer leaves. Trying to comfort it. Well, then I had to climb up higher. I flailed an arm over the greenhouse roof for support.

"And it hit me, that plant!

"It whacked me in the nose with its hard, woody branches, which ought to have been cut back who knows how long before! But they hadn't been, and there I was. So I hewed and chopped, arms dangling over the roof, chest pinned between a wall of glass and a wall of plant. 'It is a *golef*, after all,' I thought."

Elek was grinning. He could see it all perfectly clearly. He didn't know what her point was — yet he did know.

"When I was done, I climbed down the ladder through the whispering leaves, picking little, lost blossoms out of my hair, and I thought it made a curious, soft enemy, that plant, which was, of course, no enemy at all. A curious soft monster."

She stopped.

"Yes," said Elek. "Plants can be just like that."

"And people?" added Jenchae, probably concerned that Elek was failing to grasp the metaphor.

"Everything's like that," Elek said, mainly to reassure Jenchae that he'd got it.

"They're not really enemies," murmured Meravyn, "all those enemies out there."

"Oh yes. They are," said Elek. "But that's all right." He paused, searching for more proper words, but could only repeat, "It's all right."

No one answered him. They sat for a time by that black curtain stirred only by the three of them breathing. Even the ventilator's hum had stopped. The moment Elek realized it, the air seemed to grow closer. There was an electricity in it, as if life at the point of death was a rod to call down lightning.

Without warning, the floor pitched downward. A scraping noise, like a veiled scream, came from the right. They clutched each other. A deafening boom echoed above them; the floor shuddered and dipped. Slipping on the slick tiles, Elek

could feel Jenchae slide away, unable to use his hands to hold
on. Meravyn's hand was now tight in Elek's. The ground fell
beneath them, heaved back. And then her hand, too, was gone.
He groped for her. Then the impact came, so sudden and violent
it reduced the world to thunder.

CHAPTER NINETEEN

> Life is light in the darkness.
> And light will meet light.
> And the Sundering will be no more.
> This is the Shonac, the Golden Way.*
>
> The Exvocation of the Shonac, pre-10,000 B.E.

When Elek awoke, he was lying on his back, shivering, his head pounding so fiercely he doubted he could lift it. He would have preferred to go back to sleep, but the cold was overpowering. When he tried to remember what had happened, he was struck by the sense that his life in the cell had been one vast hallucination.

Inhaling deeply, he opened his eyes — and gasped as the pain in his head redoubled. Shapes floated before him, black, gray, and ice-blue. He blinked until the pain receded and the shapes resolved themselves into recognizable objects: a wall joining a ceiling, a lamp, dull and lifeless. Yet there was light, wintry, paler than the honeyed glow of the lamps.

After lying still for several seconds, gauging his position in the cell, he steeled himself and turned to face the door. Flame lanced through his head; for what seemed hours, he was aware of nothing else.

Gradually, the cell swam back into focus. Red. A blot of red on the floor. Was it —?

---

* The Exvocation is the traditional closing of the Shonac service, promising hope for the eventual unification of the universe.
Author's Note.

The standard Dabunè reads:
Fen to alno'd autsa.
Ee staltol alno alnar.
Ee d'aton deön detson Seeändo.
Os to Shonac.

Translator's Note.

His water cup, he realized with a start. He and Meravyn had played catch with it once and never returned it to the wall-box. By the cup, black floor and pale gray beyond. The door was open, perhaps the result of a power surge. The milky light stealing in from the corridor was wholly different from the strong, white fluorescence of the hall lights. Planetary light? And what planet? Elek had seen enough of the ship's layout on his march to this cell to know that there was no outer hatch in the hall — was there a hull breach then? He would have to pull himself up and investigate.

He would also have to find Jenchae and Meravyn; his chest constricted at the thought. He paused, closed his eyes and reached out his mind toward the two of them. There was nothing.

Opening his eyes, he struggled onto his elbows, then to a sitting position. The first thing his swimming gaze fell on was Jenchae. He lay in the far corner, so many bones shattered that he barely retained human shape. The pool of blood that surrounded him was already drying, his brown skin taking on a grayish hue. Elek felt nothing. He was not sure he wished to. He crawled to Jenchae's side and sat on his knees in the blood. He almost reached out to touch the crushed body but held back, wondering if Jenchae had died happy as he'd once told Elek his mother had.

No, of course, he hadn't died happy.

For a time, he knelt there, then turned to scan the rest of the room. Meravyn sprawled by the cot. Elek clambered to her side and nudged her shoulder.

"Meravyn," he called softly. She was a Tral after all, her bones and body not weak like Jenchae's. She should have survived; he had.

But when he felt for her pulse, she was cold and still. A broken puppet, she lay there askew, her head tilted at an impossible angle. Yet no more than a few hours before, her heart had pounded, her lungs heaved. She had wound her arm through his and spoken with a desperate will to survive. Now she was gone, and he went on. It was an abomination, Ned'yem's blood in the dust.

Futile. They had all known they were soon to die. Weariness descended on him. He stilled like a wind-swept room when the doors are shut.

"Meravyn, you shouldn't have let it end this way."

He stared at her, his face, his thoughts, incapable of expression. It struck him that kneeling there among the corpses, he must look like a madman. Perhaps he was one. The idea amused him mildly, and he smiled. The notion of sitting in the midst of this wreckage, smiling, amused him more, and he began to laugh. A pang shot through his neck, but that only made him laugh harder. He laughed until he was bent double, unable to breathe, till it dawned on him that his laughing was nothing more than weeping. That realization stopped his sobs, and he sat once more silent.

Absently, he noted that the pain in his neck was fading.

He looked at Meravyn again. "There's still one thing," he said. "I didn't kill you." Tears stung his eyes as he took her hand and kissed her cold forehead.

At length, shivering again, he laid her hand on her chest and heaved himself to his feet. With no clear purpose, he stumbled to the door and peered into the corridor. All the doors were open, no sign of anyone. He crept into the hall, watching, listening. Cautiously, he explored the cells, each identical to his own. Each had two or three prisoners inside, as plainly pulverized as Jenchae. He did not look closer.

At the end of the corridor was a room from which the light shone faintly brighter. He padded down the hall, leaning against the wall for support. The bright room was a guard's monitoring station. The light poured though a large gash in the hull: roughly circular, big enough for a person to climb through. Melted metal had solidified into twisted, organic shapes, canted inward. Something had burned through into the ship.

Elek shivered. The air around him breathed, swirling with life as only planetary atmospheres lived. The glow was weak and wavering. Through the breach, he could see a horizon: gray, distant mountains, swathed in mist, climbing away into clouds a paler gray. Nearer, rock, grass, scraggly trees, trunks strewn like dismembered limbs among black ashes.

A bird twilled in an airy voice. The cold pierced him to the bone.

It was too much. Like falling off a cliff into open sky. Everything clashed and clattered: the air, the cold, the birds, clouds, ground, trees. He sank to the floor, shut his eyes, waited for his brain to stop spinning. Gradually, the vertigo passed, his senses adjusted enough for him to look on the planet with a rational eye.

Atmosphere, vegetation far as the eye could see — and animal life: the birds. This world had ecosystems. Maybe a full independent biosphere. How long had they been in that cell? They could have been sent anywhere. But, no, an Ash'torian ship would only carry them within Ash'torian or Outlier space. And within that space, the vast majority of planets were ecologically degraded. Manyrock had a biosphere, but a glance showed this was not Manyrock. The Trae'dah? Back to the seat of Ash'torian power? What Trae'dah world might look like this: R'Aej? But if this were a Trae'dah world, any secure Ash'torian world, the Ash'torian authorities would be everywhere in force. An Outlying world then. That left only two possibilities: Fudûn or Yorûn, Jenchae's homeworld.

How apt if Jenchae's world became our Quol'shab, his Quol'shab. His world of birth and death.

But from what Elek knew of Yorûn, it was mostly city. Could it possibly have such mountains stretching up like living giants? Fudûn probably.

Elek made himself stop shivering. He embraced the cold seeping under his skin and stepped closer to the gap in the hull, eyes tied to the far-off horizon. Then, at the periphery of his vision, he caught sight of a mound in the corner, too soft-edged to be part of the ship.

A body. A woman's body. An officer's body, smashed, like Jenchae's. A peculiar sensation of perplexity washed over him, as if he had reached a crux but could not see the lines that made the cross. He stood as if he could substitute inactivity for thought. All at once, he moved quickly to the officer's body and searched her crushed flesh with a practiced efficiency. Her gun was still strapped at her side. He tugged it off of her belt and balanced it in his hand.

Suddenly, the cold and the pounding in his head sliced into him with renewed savagery. No thoughts would come. Once again, he stretched out his consciousness, wider now, as wide as he could. Still half expecting to feel Meravyn and Jenchae, he met a distant, unreadable flicker of strangers.

He began to speak softly, the words coming unbidden. "To live is to kill. To die is to let live." To live was also to confront life; to die, to be conquered by it. He had no more words. He fingered the gun. At last, coming to a decision, which he could not have articulated, he removed the dead officer's belt, strapped it round himself, and fit the gun into its holster.

He could hear voices now: faint, angry. He climbed through the rent in the hull and dropped onto the scorched earth below. The sky was whiter now, the world compiled of thick shadows and tinted highlights, blurring into one another. A blush above the muted land, the clouds glided over him: impossible to think that the tortured prison ship had burned through that sky only hours before. The twilling birds were calling in greater numbers now, and some other animal, an insect or another bird, that repeated a single, high chirp. Beyond them, human chatter, like rattling gourds.

His first instinct was to get away. But he had to find out what had happened, what sort of situation he had fallen into. He edged down the still-warm hull heat-warped by the ship's fiery descent, the reds and blues of its outercoat melted gray. Down the prison quarters, he inched, around the vast curve of the ship's rippling-coils, toward the voices. Hugging the hull, he could count fifteen people some way off, the outline of a small light-ship behind them. One woman, perched high on a scrap of rubble was doing her utmost to pacify the others.

"No, it hasn't been a waste," she was answering someone in heavily accented Ash'torian. "The Ash'torians have one less ship, several less officers —"

A bitter laugh in the crowd: "Yeh, we've got them round the jugular now."

"We've shown them," the leader continued, "that we can do more than just to destroy their ships. We can disable them and herd them wherever we want them to go."

"But she's still dead," came a strident voice.

"I know that this —"

"We killed her," the same voice interrupted.

Meravyn, Elek's mind whispered.

"She'd be dead if we'd done nothing anyway," the leader answered.

"Doesn't change the facts, Tarnen!" someone else shouted.

Every instinct told Elek not to go closer. *Don't put yourself in the way of this fight.* He turned and started back the way he'd come, the Strivers' voices a buzz behind him. Rounding a fragment of a focus-dish that had been blasted away from the ship, he came face to face with an Ash'torian guard. At the sight of Elek, the man staggered back, eyes wide. One arm hung useless at his side. With his other arm, he raised his gun.

At the same instant, Elek drew and fired. The gun hummed, a vibration in his hand, too low to carry to the bickering Strivers. The man jolted to the ground, shook for a second and was still. Elek felt his pulse quicken. A familiar hardness stole across his features as he gazed at the body. He was a survivor, he reflected, and this would always be the only path to survival. He stood that way a long while.

And then, something melted, quick as frost in the sun; he thought he would cry. He clipped the gun onto the belt and turned to face the ship. Pressing his palms against the hull, he closed his eyes and leaned forward until his forehead too was pressed against it. Its ebbing warmth radiated into him. He concentrated on his breathing, slowing it, slowing his heart rate as Jenchae had taught him.

Jenchae? He'd known those tricks before Jenchae had shown them. Yet now, somehow, he thought of them as Jenchae's. Perhaps that was why they worked.

Feeling sick, Elek took a deep breath and stepped away from the ship. Circumventing the guard's body, he moved on, taking care to keep the ship between himself and the Strivers — he could not involve himself with them as he had with Naquel. He was safer alone. Everyone was safer when he was alone. He looked at the ground as he walked, watching charred turf give way to untrammeled grass, grass to lichen-encrusted rock. Up on higher rocks he went, drawn by a distant rustling and a crispness in the air. Now the rocks were darker, violet and maroon, cut by wind and rain into jagged flakes. As he crossed over the apex of a boulder, he felt a rush of heat upon his face.

He looked up into the bright blue sky, past the sun that was opening its eye over the ocean. Down he looked, into the sky-colored waters that lapped lazily at weathered stones on a beach perhaps twenty meters below. He sat on the splintered cliff, gazed over the flashing sea, breathed the salt air.

While the sun climbed, Elek's eye wandered almost placid over waves and shore and up to the rough rock he sat on. It looked like an old man's hand — Jenchae's hand — deep, veiny tracks carved out where minerals had dissolved: maroon lines, brown, violet, white, a minute mountain range for the little black crustaceans climbing busily up and down. He wondered how this rock had come to rise above the sea. He wondered at the intricacy of its mineral trails, the tiny flakes he brushed with his fingers, the sun warm, the grinding tides. How many more thousand sensory impressions than the black tiles of the cell and whistle of the ventilator. He shuddered at the memory.

That had been the deathland; this was the rebirth. But Meravyn and Jenchae had passed into the dark. If there were justice in this universe, it would have been him. He was the natural choice for death, the only one of the three who deserved it. Yet they were gone, and the most vicious part of all was that he did not even feel much sorrow. They were gone — no more than a few hours gone — and he was here happy to be sitting in the sun above the ocean. That was monstrous. He was monstrous. All their care for him had been in vain because he would never be a real person, never feel as people should.

He thought of Ned'yem, her arms outstretched, bleeding into the dust. And he understood it suddenly: grief's need to bleed outside as in. Glancing around, he spotted a jutting shard of rock. He edged over to it and rolled up his sleeve, scraped his forearm hard across it. The pain was a restoration of rightness. One gash for Jenchae and Meravyn both.

He watched the blood flow down his arm over his hand, contemplated the stinging. And over the pain, the sun soaked tranquilly into his hands.

It could not be for nothing. He had a duty to remember them, to tell others of their lives and deaths. He owed it them to live well. They had believed he was going to die, yet they had treated him as a being with a future. Was that foolish? Naive instinct? It had come to pass, at any rate. They were gone, but he was here alive and out of the hands of Ash'tor. He could not — he would not — betray their faith. He would live —

He would believe —

No, he would know —

Well, he would *hope* that he could exist as a person among other people. Was that possible? To be part of a society again?

Not to kill —?

He thought of the Ash'torian guard, and his gut clenched.

— except when life demands killing. But had it then? Would the guard have shot him? Could they have talked? No. That was ridiculous. The universe was as vicious as ever, and living demanded killing.

Yet. . . if he could learn to kill only in need, then that would mean a great deal. And he would. He could. He must, in memory of them. He would carry them with him.

A memory of Naquel kindled in him, of their first meeting, years ago, when he had found Naquel bleeding in the desert and taken him in and bandaged him. "You could return to the world," the Striver leader had said. "You have it in you to return — to aid your people." Naquel had been wrong then, but now Elek would make it true. He would have to go to the Strivers, be with others, for life was made of other lives, as a rope was made of threads twined together.

As he stood, the sun pulsed warm on his black coverall and, higher now, followed him warm down the rocky path. The wreckage of the ship glinted, bright and solid, almost as beautiful as an old tree's sun-bleached skeleton.

He was still some meters from the ship when a Striver, rounding the wreck, caught sight of him. The man lifted his gun at once.

Elek halted, raised his empty hands. "I'm a friend; I'm a friend," he called in Ash'torian. "I was a prisoner on the ship." His prison clothes and his Tral face should validate that.

The man, quite young, approached him, gun still raised. "How did you live?" he asked, his own Ash'torian slow and labored.

"Sverra," said Elek.

"Why were you in prison?" the man asked, eyes narrow.

"Rebellion," Elek lied. "Look, I'm a Manyrocker; I have no love for Ash'tor." Elek's thoughts bounded on as he spoke. Of course, Naquel could identify him as a murderer. But Naquel had bigger ripples to cast; he'd assume Elek was dead and think no more of him. And the relative absence of visual records among both Ash'torians and Outliers made it unlikely he'd be recognized. Yes, Elek could manage it, start a new way of living. "My name is Brec," he told the Outlier.

The man eyed him a moment more. "Fojec." He gave his own name with an air of decision and lowered his gun.

"So what happened here?"

Fojec sniffed. "Biggest debacle I've ever been party to," he said, slipping into an Ash'torian-Dab patois. "Far too complex of a plan to ever come off, if you ask me. We were out to rescue, well, anyone we could but mainly Soro, you know?"

"I've heard of her."

"Well, sure. She's one of the biggest names."

"She was on this ship?"

"Was. She's dead now. We attacked them in mid-space."

"I felt it," Elek answered and smiled. "Twice."

"Yeh, the first time, our people managed to board and take out the coms and lock navigation a course for Fudûn. But then, the Ash'torians chopped up our attack force. So there was the ship, helpless. Good. But none of our people left on the inside, or even rippling close to the ship. Not so good."

"It took the ship a long time to get here," said Elek.

Fojec threw him a noncommittal look. "Not really," he answered. "Six days. That's about as direct as you can get." He grinned. "Guess it feels longer on the inside."

"I guess so." Only six days? Only six days he'd known Meravyn. And that would be — what? — eight? nine? he'd known Jenchae?

"Anyway," Fojec was saying, "they got here, where we wanted them, but with none of our people left alive — or free at least — on board, we couldn't make them land. Tried to disable them, force a soft landing. But some god-scoffing pilot managed to thrash our attack. Instead the damn ship crashes. You know, you may be the only survivor."

The only survivor. A wave of indignation passed through Elek.

A botched attack. They were trying to rescue us, but they killed us — everyone but me. Gods! They should have just let us go to execution! At least they'd have seen the sun again, Meravyn and Jenchae. They'd have seen the sky.

Instead, these clumsy fools had robbed them even of that. Elek could feel his right arm tense. How easy it would be to reach out and crush this boy before him.

Idiotic, grinning boy. This rough-hewn, Sama boy — so young, and doomed to a life of fighting. No, Elek didn't want to crush him, this blue-eyed child so weirdly trusting of a stranger he'd just met. Before long, that trust would be beaten out of him.

But not by me.

Elek sighed.

An attack gone wrong, and you don't mean to kill but you do it. That happened to Meravyn. It's happened to me. To these fighters here. To Ash'tor. To all of us.

"Have you heard of Denned Jenchae?" It wasn't a wise thing to say, but Elek was still angry enough to feel compelled to say it.

"Working out of Taenquûn?" Fojec said.

Elek nodded. "He was my cellmate. Didn't make it."

"Damn," said Fojec.

"I couldn't have put it better."

Fojec was silent a moment. "Makes you feel like giving in, handing in your gun."

"It sure does," Elek agreed. But Jenchae would not want that. Meravyn wouldn't.

Fojec sighed and straightened. "You'd best come with us for now."

"It's better than a prison ship."

They began to walk toward the knot of Strivers who were staring at them now.

"Are you going to head back to Manyrock?" Fojec asked.

"Maybe," said Elek, surprised by a surge of longing. He could almost feel the warm sun of the Manyrock winter. To go back to Manyrock and find somewhere where nobody remembered him and he could try again, live again, harvest again in the marula groves — groves exploited by Ash'tor now, Meravyn had said — but that didn't matter. Someone was always exploiting something. The coarse, friendly touch of the tree limbs would remain. And he'd be there, be home. Find Meravyn's sister? Tell her how much he owed Meravyn? Perhaps that would reopen too many wounds. Yet perhaps they needed to be reopened, there in the clean, healing air washed dry by the sun.

But Manyrock's sun was only one of hundreds. Even now, the sun was beating into his bones. It was already here. It was everywhere.

TRANSLATOR'S NOTE TO THE FIRST VUNIZH EDITION

"Our peoples, bereft of their planet of origin, were bereft as well in their millennia of wandering of the unifying society which that world represented. Such peoples must continually be searching for a center, an axis around which to order their flowering." So wrote Bra'hem T'Ah'ré Qhe'byq in the preface to the original Ash'torian edition of *The Hour before Morning* (year 2140 After the End). "I have set down this tale as I heard it," she claimed. "To my mind, it is the essence of this search in small." I wonder.

'Eblia Te'Zhano Yor, 2165 A.E.

www.ingramcontent.com/pod-product-compliance
Lightning Source LLC
Chambersburg PA
CBHW050331110726
47899CB00007B/2450